ADE'S FABLES

GEORGE ADE

1st WORLD
LIBRARY
Literary Society

Ade's Fables

George Ade

© 1st World Library, 2006
PO Box 2211
Fairfield, IA 52556
www.1stworldlibrary.com
First Edition

LCCN: 2007920644

Softcover ISBN: 978-1-4218-3954-7
Hardcover ISBN: 978-1-4218-3854-0
eBook ISBN: 978-1-4218-4054-3

Purchase *"Ade's Fables"*
as a traditional bound book at:
www.1stWorldLibrary.com/purchase.asp?ISBN=978-1-4218-3954-7

1st World Library is a literary, educational organization
dedicated to:

- Creating a free internet library of downloadable ebooks

- Hosting writing competitions and offering book
  publishing scholarships.

Interested in more 1st World Library books?
contact: literacy@1stworldlibrary.com
Check us out at: www.1stworldlibrary.com

1st World Library Literary Society

Giving Back to the World

"If you want to work on the core problem, it's early school literacy."

- James Barksdale, former CEO of Netscape

"No skill is more crucial to the future of a child, or to a democratic and prosperous society, than literacy."

- Los Angeles Times

Literacy... means far more than learning how to read and write... The aim is to transmit... knowledge and promote social participation."

- UNESCO

"Literacy is not a luxury, it is a right and a responsibility. If our world is to meet the challenges of the twenty-first century we must harness the energy and creativity of all our citizens."

- President Bill Clinton

"Parents should be encouraged to read to their children, and teachers should be equipped with all available techniques for teaching literacy, so the varying needs and capacities of individual kids can be taken into account."

- Hugh Mackay

CONTENTS

The New Fable of the Private Agitator and
What He Cooked Up.. 7

The New Fable of the Speedy Sprite 17

The New Fable of the Intermittent Fusser.................... 26

The New Fable of the Search for Climate..................... 35

The New Fable of the Father Who Jumped In 44

The New Fable of the Uplifter and
His Dandy Little Opus.. 53

The New Fable of the Wandering Boy
and the Wayward Parent... 62

The New Fable of What Transpires
After the Wind-up 72

The Dream That Came Out with Much to Boot 80

The New Fable of the Toilsome Ascent and
the Shining Table-Land 88

The New Fable of the Aerial Performer, the Buzzing
Blondine, and the Daughter of Mr. Jackson 98

The New Fable of Susan and the Daughter and the
Granddaughter, and then Something Really Grand....108

The New Fable of the Scoffer Who Fell Hard
and the Woman Sitting By...120

The New Fable of the Lonesome Camp on
the Frozen Heights..130

The New Fable of the Marathon in the Mud
and the Laurel Wreath 141

THE NEW FABLE OF THE PRIVATE AGITATOR AND WHAT HE COOKED UP

Ambition came, with Sterling Silver Breast-Plate and Flaming Sword, and sat beside a Tad aged 5. The wee Hopeful lived in a Frame House with Box Pillars in front and Hollyhocks leading down toward the Pike.

"Whither shall I guide you?" asked Ambition. "Are you far enough from the Shell to have any definite Hankering?"

"I have spent many Hours brooding over the possibilities of the Future," replied the Larva. "I want to grow up to be a Joey in a Circus. I fairly ache to sit in a Red Wagon just behind the Band and drive a Trick Mule with little pieces of Looking Glass in the Harness. I want to pull Mugs at all the scared Country Girls peeking out of the Wagon Beds. The Town Boys will leave the Elephant and trail behind my comical Chariot. In my Hour of Triumph the Air will be impregnated with Calliope Music and the Smell of Pop-Corn, modified by Wild Animals."

Ambition went out to make the proper Bookings with Destiny. When he came back the Boy was ten years old.

"We started wrong," whispered Ambition, curling up in the cool grass near the Day-Dreamer. "The Trick Mule and the Red Cart are all very well for little Fraidy-Cats and Softies, but a brave Youth of High Spirit should tread the Deck of his own Ship with a Cutlass under his Red Sash. Aye, that is Blood gauming up the Scuppers, but is the Captain chicken-hearted? Up with the Black Flag! Let it be give and take, with Pieces of Eight for the Victor!"

So it was settled that the Lad was to hurry through the Graded Schools and then get at his Buccaneering.

But Ambition came back with a revised Program. "You are now Fifteen Years of Age," said the Wonderful Guide with the glittering Suit. "It is High Time that you planned a Noble Career, following a Straight Course from which there shall be no Deviation. The Pirate is a mere swaggering Bravo and almost Unscrupulous at times. Why not be a great Military Commander? The Procedure is Simple. Your Father gives the Finger to the Congressman and then you step off the Boat at West Point. Next thing you know, you are wearing a Nobby Uniform right out on the Parade Ground, while bevies of Debutantes from New York City and other Points admire you for the stern Profile and Military Set-Up. After that you will subdue many Savage Tribes, and then you will march up Pennsylvania Avenue at the head of the whole Regular Army, and the President of the United States will be waiting on the Front Porch of the White House to present you with a jewelled Sword on behalf of a Grateful Nation."

"You are right," said the Stripling. His eyes were like Saucers, and his Nostrils quivered. "I will be Commander-in-Chief, and after I am laid away, with the Cannon booming, the Folks in this very Town will put up a Statue of Me at the corner of Sixth and Main, so the Street-Cars will have to circle to get around it."

Consequently, when he was in his 21st Year, he was sitting at a high Desk in an Office watching the Birds on a Telegraph Wire. The Knowledge he had acquired at the two Prep Schools before being pushed into the Fresh Air ahead of Time had not made him round-shouldered.

He was a likely Chap, but he wore no Plumes.

George Ade

He became dimly conscious that Ambition was squatted on the Stool next to him.

"Up to this time we have been Dead Wrong," said the Periodical Visitor. "There is only one Prize worth winning and that is the Love of the Niftiest Nectarine that ever came down a Crystal Stairway from the Celestial Regions to grace this dreary World with her Holy Presence. Yes, I mean the One you passed this morning—the One with her hair in a Net and the Cameo Brooch. Why not annex her by Legal Routine and settle down in a neat Cottage purchased from the Building and Loan Association? You could raise your own Vegetables. Go to it."

Four years elapse. Our Hero now has everything. The jerry-built home of the Early Bungalow Period stands up bravely under the Mortgage. Little Dorothy is suspended in a Jump Chair on the Veranda facing Myrtle Avenue, along which the Green Cars run direct to City Hall Square. The Goddess is in the kitchen trying to make preserves out of Watermelon Rinds, with the White House Cook Book propped open in front of her. Friend Husband is weeding the Azaleas and grieving over the failure of the Egg-Plant.

He finds himself gently prodded, and there is Ambition once more at his Elbow.

"You are entitled to One Hundred Thousand Dollars," murmurs the stealthy Promoter. "Why should some other Citizen have his Coal-Bin right in his House while you carry it from a Shed? Your Wife should sit at her own Dinner Table and make signs at the Maid. And as you ride to your Work with the other dead-eyed Cattle and see all those Strong-Arm Johnnies coming out of their Brick Mansions to hop into their own Broughams and Coupes, have you not asked yourself why you are in the Horse-Cars with the Plebes when you might be in a Private Rig with the Patricians?"

For, wot ye, Gentle Reader, all this unwound from the Reel

before the first Trolley Car climbed a Hill or the first Horseless Carriage came chugging sternly up the Boulevard.

So Ambition received special Instructions to make Our Hero worth $100,000.

Those were the day of tall Hustling: If he saw an Opening six inches wide, he held it with his Foot until he could insert his Elbow, and then he braced his Shoulder, and the first thing you knew he was on the Inside demanding a fair cut of the Swag.

The Golden Rule received many a Jolt, but he adhered strictly to the old and favorite Admonition: If you want Yours, take a short piece of Lead Pipe and go out and Collect.

On a certain January First he made a careful Invoice. All the Hard-Earned Kale dropped into the Mining Companies or loaned to Relatives of Wife he marked off and put under the Head of Gone but not Forgotten. He was a True Business Guy. Even after subtracting all Cats and Dogs he could still total the magnificent Sum of One Hundred Thousand Dollars.

When he looked at this Mound of Currency, he felt like a Vag and a Pauper. For he had climbed to the table-lands of High Finance and taken a peek at the Steam-Roller methods of the Real Tabascos.

"Make it a Million," said Ambition, leaning across the Table and tapping nervously. "Are you going to be satisfied with a Station Wagon and a Colored Boy when you might have a long-waisted Vehicle with two pale Simpsons in Livery on the Box? When you go into your Club and see the Menials kow-towing to a cold-looking Party with rippling Chins who seems to favor his Feet, you know that he gets the Waving Palms and the Frankincense because he is a Millionaire. You and the other financial Gnats are admitted simply to make a Stage Setting for the Big Squash."

"I always said that when I got a Hundred Thousand I'd take a long Vacation in Europe and learn how to order a Meal," suggested Our Hero, holding out weakly.

"When you came back you would find your hated Rival on the Hill with the Batteries turned against you. Camp on the Job and work straight toward the High Mark. And remember that anybody with less than a Million is a Two-Spot in a soiled Deck."

From that day the Piking ceased. No more of the dinky trafficking of the Retailer. He went out and bought Public Service Utilities on Nerve, treated them with Aqua Pura by the Hogshead, and created Wealth by purely lithographic Methods. And, if he wanted to reason out a Deal with a contrary-minded Gazook, he began the Negotiations by soaking the Adversary behind the Ear and frisking him before he came to.

A Fairy Wand had been waved above the snide Bungalow, and it was now a Queen Anne Chateau dripping with Dew-dads of Scroll Work and congested with Black Walnut. The Goddess took her Mocha in the Feathers, and a Music Teacher came twice each week to bridge the awful chasm between Dorothy and Chopin. Dinner had been moved up to Milking Time. Sweetbreads and Artichokes came into the Lives of the Trio thus favored by Fortune.

One day the busy Thimble-Rigger took his Helpmate into the lonesome Library and broke the glad Tidings to her.

"I have unloaded all my Cripples," he said. "They have been wished on a Group of Philanthropists in New England. Sound the glad Tocsin. I have a Million in my Kick."

So she began packing the huge Saratogas and reading the Folders on Egypt and the Riviera. He sat in his Den pulling at a long black Excepcionale. Through the bluish clouds of Smoke came that old familiar Voice.

"Let the Missus and the Heiress do the European Thing," said Ambition. "You stick around. Wait for Black Friday. Then get busy at the Bargain Counter. By and by the new Crop will begin to move, and Money will creep out of the Yarn Stockings and a few Wise Gazabes will cop all the Plush. In every Palm Room there are more Millionaires than Palms. But the Big Round Table over by the Fountain is always reserved by Oscar for the Lad who can show Ten Millions."

The Ocean Greyhound moved out past Sandy Hook with the Family and all the Maids on board, but Papa remained behind to sharpen his Tools and get ready for another Killing.

Every time he was given a Crimp in the Rue de la Paix he caught even by leading a new Angora up the Chute and into the Shambles.

When the fully matured Goddess and the radiant Heroine of the latest International Alliance came home with the French Language and two tons of Glad Raiment, they found them selves reuning with the Magnate at the big Table over by the Fountain.

Our Hero was now sleeping in a Bed almost twelve feet wide, with a silk Tent over it. One Morning he found the Companion of many Years sitting on the edge of the Mattress.

"Again?" asked the Multi-Millionaire. "What next?"

"The Exercises up to this Time have been Preliminary," said Ambition. "What is the good of a Bank Roll if you cannot garnish it with the delectable Parsley of Social Eminence? Get a Wiggle on you. Send for the Boys with the Frock Coats and the Soft Hats and let them dig in to their Elbows. Tell the Press Agent to organize a typewriting Phalanx. Assume a few Mortgages on fluttering Newspapers. Lay a Corner-Stone ever and anon. Be Interviewed."

"What are you leading up to?" asked the Financial Giant, a

sickly Fear creeping into the Region formerly occupied by his Heart.

"The Logical Finish," replied Ambition, with a reassuring Pat on the Shoulder. "You must go to the Senate. The White Palace, suitable for entertaining purposes, now awaits you in Washington. The Bulb Lights glow dimly above the Porte Cochere. A red Carpet invites you to climb the Marble Stairway and spread yourself all over the Throne. On a Receiving Night, when the perfumed Aliens in their Masquerade Suits rally around the Punch Bowl, your Place will resemble the Last Act of something by Klaw & Erlanger. You will play Stud with the Makers of History and be seen leaving the Executive Mansion."

This Line of Talk landed him. He Fell for it. That year the Christmas Tree drooped with valuable Gifts for the Boys who stood after they were hitched.

He went up to Washington with an eviscerated Check-Book in his Pocket, and a faint Odor of Scandal in his Wake, but he was a certified Servant of the People. His Cut Flowers were the Talk in Official Circles. The most Exclusive consented to flirt with his Wine Cellar.

To a mere Outsider it looked as if Ambition had certainly boosted his Nobs to the final Himalayan Peak of Human Happiness. He had a House as big as a Hospital. The Hallways were cluttered with whispering Servants of the most immaculate and grovelling Description. His Wife and the Daughter and the Cigarette-Holder she had picked up in Europe figured in the Gay Life of the Nation's Capital every Night and went to see a Nerve Specialist every Day. The whole Bunch rode gaily on the Top Wave of the Social Swim, with a Terrapin as an Escort and a squad of Canvas-Back Ducks as Body-Guard.

Notwithstanding all which, Father was the sorest Hard-Shell that motored along Pennsylvania Avenue.

The Dime Denouncers printed his Picture, saying that he was owned by the Interests and hated the sight of a Poor Working Girl. When the High Class continuous Show in the Senate Chamber showed signs of flopping and the Press Gallery became impatient, some Alkali Statesman of the New School would arise in his Place and give our Hero a Turning-Over, concluding with a faithful Pen-Picture of the Dishonored Grave marked by a single Headstone, chiseled as follows: "Here lies a Burglar."

When he went traveling, he had his Food smuggled into the Drawing-Room. He knew if he went drilling through the Pullmans, some of the Passengers who had seen the Cartoons might recognize him as the notorious Malefactor.

One day, while he was cowering in a dark corner of his Club to get away from the pesky Reporters, he was joined by the Trouble-Maker.

"I gave you the wrong Steer," said Ambition, now much subdued. "You are in Dutch. Beat it! All the Rough-Necks down by the Round-House and the fretful Simps along every R. F. D. Route are getting ready to interfere in the Affairs of Government. The Storm Clouds of Anarchy are lowering. In other words, the new Primary Law has begun to do business. Every downtrodden Mokus owing $800 on a $500 House is honing for a Chance to Hand It to somebody wearing a Seal-Skin Overcoat. From now on, seek Contentment, Rural Quietude, and a cinch Rate of 5 Per Cent. on all your Holdings."

So Ambition, after leading him hither and yon, finally conducted him to the swell Country House surrounded by Oaks and winding Drives and Sunken Gardens.

Far from the Hurly-Burly he settled down among his Boston Terriers and Orchids and Talking-Machines and allowed Old Age to ripen and mellow him into a Patriarch of the benevolent Pattern.

At the suggestion of an expensive Specialist, he went in for Golf. After he had learned to Follow Through and keep within 100 yards of the Fair Green, he happened to get mixed up in a Twosome one day with a walking Rameses who had graduated from the Stock Exchange soon after the Crime of '73. This doddering Shell of Humanity looked as if a High Wind would blow him into the Crick. When he swung at the Pill, you expected to hear something Snap.

Our Hero had about 10 Years on the Ancient, and it looked like a Compote. But the Antique managed to totter around the Course, playing short but safe, always getting Direction and keeping away from the Profanity Pits.

He never caught up with Colonel Bogey, but he had enough Class to trim our Hero and collect 6 Balls.

Ambition rode home with the unhappy Loser in the $12,000 Limousine. "Buck up, Old Top," said the faithful Prompter. "Fasten your Eye on the Ball and don't try to Force. He is sure to blow up sooner or later. Take another Lesson to-morrow morning and then publish your Defi in the afternoon."

He never had been strong enough to stand off Ambition. So the next Day he took on Old Sure-Thing again and got it in the same Place.

No wonder. The Octogenarian was of Scotch Descent. He was the Color of an Army Saddle. He never smiled except when the Kilties came on tour. His Nippie consisted of a tall Glass about half full and then a little Well Water.

A plain American Business Man with a York State Ancestry had a fat Chance against this Caledonian frame-up.

But that same persistent Ambition kept sending him back to the Ring to take another Trouncing.

One day he failed to show up at the Club House. The Trained

Nurse, who fanned him during the final Hours, never suspected. But the Caddy- Master knew that he had died of a Broken Heart.

MORAL: Those who travel the hardest are not always the first to arrive.

THE NEW FABLE OF THE SPEEDY SPRITE

One Monday Morning a range and well-conditioned Elfin of the Young Unmarried Set, yclept Loretta, emerged into the Sunlight and hit the Concrete Path with a ringing Heel.

This uncrowned Empress of the 18th Ward was a she-Progressive assaying 98 per cent. pure Ginger.

Instead of trailing the ever onward Parade, she juggled the Baton at the head of the Push.

In the crisp introductory hours of the Wash-Day already woven into the Plot, Loretta trolleyed herself down into the Noise Belt.

She went to the office of the exclusive Kennel Club and entered the Chow Ki-Yi for the next Bench Show. At the Clearing House for K. M.'s she filed a loud call for a Cook who could cook. Then she cashed a check, ordered a pound of Salted Nuts (to be delivered by Special Wagon at once), enveloped a ball of Ice Cream gooed with Chocolate, and soon, greatly refreshed, swept down upon a Department Store.

A Chenille Massacre was in full swing on the 3d floor, just between the Porch Furniture and Special Clothing for Airmen. Loretta took a run and jump into the heaving mass of the gentler Division. She came out at 10.53 with her Sky Piece badly listed to Port and her toes flattened out, but she was 17 cents to the Good. Three hearty Cheers!

So she went over to an exhibition of Paintings, breathing through her Nose for at least an Hour as she studied the new Masterpieces of the Swedo-Scandinavian School. Each looked as if executed with a Squirt Gun by a Nervous Geek on his way to a Three Days Cure. Just the same, every Visitor with a clinging Skirt and a Mushroom Hat gurgled like a Mountain Stream.

In company with four other Seraphines, plucked from the Society Col., she toyed with a Fruit Salad and Cocoa at a Tea Room instituted by a Lady in Reduced Circumstances for the accommodation of those who are never overtaken by Hunger.

The usual Battle as to which should pick up the Check and the same old Compromise. A Dutch Treat with the Waitress trying to spread it four ways and the Auditing Committee watching her like a Hawk. Then a 10-cent Tip, bestowed as if endowing Princeton, and the Quartet representing the Flower of America's Young Womanhood was once more out in the Ozone, marching abreast with shining Faces and pushing white-haired Business Men off into the Sweepings.

Loretta went to a place with a glass Cover on it and had herself photoed in many a striking Posture. With the Chin tilted to show the full crop of Cervical Vertebrae and her Search Lights aimed yearningly at the top of the Singer Building, she had herself kidded into believing that she was a certified Replica of Elsie Ferguson.

As a member of the Board of Visitation she hurried out to the Colored Orphan Asylum to check up the Picks and watch them making Card-Board Mottoes.

After that she had nothing to do except fly home and complete a Paper on the Social Unrest in Spain, after which she backed into the Spangles, because Father was bringing an old Stable Companion to dinner.

In the evening she took Mother to a Travel Lecture. The

colored Slides were mingled with St. Vitus Glimpses of swarming Streets and galloping Gee-Gees. They came home google-eyed and had to feel their way into the Domicile.

Tuesday A. M. dawned overcast with shifting winds from the N. E.. Loretta pried herself away from the third Waffle in order to hike to the corner and jack up Mr. Grocer about the Kindling Wood that he had sent them for Celery.

She had the Druggist 'phone the Florist, and then rewarded him by purchasing three Stamps.

At 9.30 the Committee to arrange for the Summer Camp of the In-Wrong Married Women whirled through the untidy Suburbs in a next year's Motor Car, and Loretta was nowhere except right up on the front Seat picking out the Road.

Once a year the Ladies of the Lumty-Tum went out with their embroidered Sand-Bags and swung on their Gentlemen Friends for enough Dough to pay the Vacation Expenses of Neglected Wives and Kiddies.

In every community there is an undiscovered Triton thoroughly posted on the Renaissance of the Reactionaries and the recrudescence of the Big Six Baby with the up-twist that has the Whiskers on it. This Boy is so busy regulating both Parties and both Leagues that when it comes time for his Brood to take an Outing, some ignorant Outsider has to step in and unbelt.

After letting contracts for Milk and Vegetables, Loretta and the other specimens of our Best People zipped over to the Country Club, breaking into silvery Laughter every time the Speedometer made a Face at the Sign-Board which said that the Speed Limit was 12 Miles an Hour.

They showed a few milk-fed Springers how to take a Joke, and then played an 18-hole Foursome which was more or less of a Grewsome.

Then a little Tea on the Terrace with Herbert lolling by in his Flannels, just as you read about it in Mrs. Humphrey Ward.

A buzzing sound dying off into the distance, a trail of Blue Smoke in the fading Twilight, and little Bright Eyes is back in her own Boudoir packing herself into a new set of Glads.

That evening she had four throbbing Roscoes curled up among her Sofa Pillows.

She had to bat up short and easy ones for this Bunch, as they came from the Wholesale District.

When they began to distribute political Bromides, the artful Minx sat clear out on the edge of the Chair and let on to be simply pop-eyed with Ardor.

Shortly after 12 she turned the last night-blooming Cyril out into the Darkness and did a graceful Pirouet to the Husks.

On Wednesday morning, between the Ham and Eggs, she glanced at her double-entry Date Book and began to gyrate.

On the way down-town she stopped in and had herself measured for a new mop of hair.

Thence to the Beauty Works to have the peerless Frontispiece ironed out and the Nails ivoried.

When she appeared at the Sorority Tiffin at 1 P. M. she was dolled for fair.

The Response in behalf of the Alumnae of Yamma Gamma was a neat Affair. After swiping the Table Decorations, she and two Companions hurried to a Mat. It was a Performance given under the auspices of the Overhanging Domes, and the Drama was one that no Commercial Manager had the Nerve to unload on the Public. The Plot consisted of two victims of

George Ade

Neurasthenia sitting at a Table and discussing Impaired Circulation.

That evening she helped administer the Anesthetic to a Seminary Snipe who was getting into the Life Boat with a hard-wood Bachelor grabbed off at the 11th Hour.

Loretta wept softly while straightening out the Veil, in accordance with Tradition. Later on she did an Eddie Collins and landed the Bride's Bouquet. At 11.30 she had the Best Man backed into a Corner, slipping him that Old One about his Hair matching his Eyes.

It is now Thursday morning and who is this in the Gym whanging the Medicine Ball at the Lady Instructor with the Face?

It is Loretta.

Behold her at 10.30, after an icy Splash and a keen rub with a raspy Towel.

She has climbed back into the dark-cloth Effect and is headed for the Studio of Madam to grapple with the French Lesson.

After that she will do nothing before Lunch Time except try on White Shoes and fondle some Hats that are being sacrificed at $80 per throw.

The Suffrage Sisters rounded up Thursday afternoon. A longitudinal Brigadieress in the army of Intellectuality did the main Spiel, with Loretta as principal Rooter.

The Speaker was there with the Pep and with the Vocabulary. Otherwise she was a Naughty-Naughty. The costume was a plain Burial Shroud, the only Ornament being a 4-carat Wen just above the Neck-band.

At 4 P. M., after the Male Sex had been ground to a

Hamburger, our little Playmate escaped to a Picture Show, but not until she had duly fortified herself with the nourishing Marshmallow.

There was nothing on the Cards that night except a Subscription Dance, which got under way at 10 P. M. and never subsided until the cold Daylight began to spill in at the Windows.

Loretta did a 27 out of a possible 29. Percentage .931—six better than Bogey and 400 points ahead of Ty Cobb.

Nevertheless and notwithstanding, don't imagine that she failed to come up for Air on Friday Morning.

Life is real, Life is earnest, and she had a Gown to be shortened upand re-surveyed around the Horse Shoe Curve, just as soon as she could leave the Gloves to be cleaned.

Happening into Automobile Row, she permitted a blond salesman with a Norfolk Jacket to demonstrate the new type of Electric Runabout.

One of the most inexpensive pursuits of the well-dressed Minority is to glide over the Asphalt in a Demonstration Car and pretend to be undecided.

She permitted the man to set her down at a Book Shop, where she furtively skinned eight Magazines while waiting for a Chum to pop through the Whirligig Door.

The two went Window-Hopping for an hour. After making Mind Purchases of about $8000 worth of washable Finery edged with Lace, a spirit of Deviltry seized them.

They ordered their Lettuce Sandwiches and diluted Ceylon in a Restaurant where roguish Men-about-Town sat facing the Main Entrance to pipe the pulchritudinous Pippins.

Was it seven or eight Party Calls that she checked from her social Ledger before 4 o'clock? Answer: eight.

Then a swinging Gallop for home. Whilst she had been socializing around, Robert W. Chambers had taken a lead of two Novels on her. Retiring to a quiet Alcove with four Volumes that were being dissected at the drawing-room Clinics, she took a hack at the first and last Chapter of each. Just enough to protect her against a Fumble if she found herself next to a Book Sharp.

That evening a famous Hungarian Fiddler, accompanied by a warbling Guinea Hen and backed up by sixty Symphonic Heineys wearing Spectacles, was giving a Recital for the True Lovers in a Mammoth Cave devoted to Art.

Loretta had a sneaking preference for the May Irwin School of Expression, but she had to go through with the Saint-Saens Stuff now and then to maintain a Club Standing.

Accordingly she and Mother and poor old dying Father, with no Heart in the Enterprise, were planted well down in Section B, where they could watch Mrs. Leroy Geblotz, who once entertained Nordica, and say "Bravo" at the Psychological Moment.

On Saturday Morning, after she had penned 14 Epistles, using the tall cuneiform Hieroglyphics, she didn't have a blessed thing to do before her 1 o'clock Engagement except drop in at a Flower Show and a Cat Show and have her Palm read by a perfectly fascinating Serpent with a Goatee who had been telling all the Gells the most wonderful things about themselves.

A merry little Group went slumming Saturday afternoon. They attended a Ball Game. Loretta had her Chin over the Railing and evinced a keen Interest, her only Difficulty being that she never knew which Side was at bat.

At dusk she began hanging on the Family Jewels. It was a formal Dinner Party with a list made up by Dun and Bradstreet.

Loretta found herself between an extinct Volcano of Political World and a sappy Fledgling whose Grandfather laid the cornerstone of Brooklyn.

The Dinner was one of those corpseless Funerals, stage-managed by a respectable Lady with a granite Front who had Mayflower Corpuscles moving majestically through her Arterial System.

Loretta was marooned so far from the Live Ones that she couldn't wig-wag for Help. Her C. Q. D. brought no Relief.

She threw about three throes of Anguish before they escaped to the private Gambling Hell.

Here she tucked back her Valenciennes and proceeded to cop a little Pin-Money at the soul-destroying game known as Bridge.

At 11.30 she led a highly connected volunteer Wine Pusher out into the Conservatory and told him she did not think it advisable to marry him until she had learned his First Name.

Shortly after Midnight she blew, arriving at headquarters just in time to participate in a Chafing-Dish Jubilee promoted by only Brother, just back from the Varsity.

She approached the Porcelain in a chastened mood that Sabbath morning. She was thinking of the Night Before and of playing cards for Money. She remembered the glare of Light for overhead and the tense, eager Faces peering above the Paste-Boards.

Then she recalled, with a sharp catch of the Breath and a little tug of Pain at the Heart, that she had balled herself up at one Stage and got dummied out of a Grand Slam.

"It would have meant a long pair of the Silk Kind," thought she, as she sighed deeply and turned the cold Faucet.

After Breakfast, she took a long Walk up the Avenue as a Bracer.

After which to the Kirk, for she taught a class of Little Girls in the Sunday School, and she had to fake up an Explanation of how Joshua made the Sun stand still, thereby putting herself in the Scratch Division of Explainers, believe us.

She listened to a dainty Boston Sermon, trimmed with Ruching, singing lustily before and after.

Then back home with the solemn Parade to sit among the condemned waiting for that superlative Gorge known as the Sunday Dinner.

While she was waiting, a male Friend dropped in. His costume was a compromise between an English Actor and a hired Mourner.

On Week Days he sat at a Desk dictating Letters and saying that the Matter had been referred to the proper Department.

He looked at Loretta, so calm and cool and collected in her pious Raiment, and the Smile that he summoned was benevolent and almost patronizing.

"I was wondering," said he. "I was wondering if a Girl like you ever gets tired of sitting around and doing nothing."

Loretta did not cackle. She had read in a Book by a Yale Professor that Woman is not supposed to possess the Sense of Humor.

MORAL: The Settlement Campaign is not getting to the real Workers.

THE NEW FABLE OF THE INTERMITTENT FUSSER

Once a grammar-school Rabbit, struggling from long Trousers toward his first brier-wood Pipe, had Growing Pains which he diagnosed as the pangs of True Love.

The Target was a dry-seasoned Fannie old enough to be his Godmother. She was a Post-Graduate who was keeping herself on Earth by running to the Drug-Store every few minutes.

The Eye-Brows were neatly blocked out by some Process unknown to the writer, and she had a Shape that could be revised ad lib.

An Expert would have Made her at a glance, but the Cub fell for the Scenery and Mechanical Effects.

He had sketched a little synopsis of the Future. After waiting 8 years, until she had unpetaled into the perfect bloom of Womanhood and he was wearing a Full Beard, he would take her by the Long Glove and lead her off into Dreamland.

Just to show how one of those pinfeather Passions may be shunted onto a Siding and left among the Dog-Fennel, when the Subject of this Sketch was *aetat* 22, he was picking them out of the Air in the Left Garden at the State University. Fannie (she of the purchased Pallor) was thoroughly married to a Veterinary with the Drug Habit.

Soon after recovering from the Pip, known in Medical

Parlance as the Spooney Infantum, he began to glory in the friendship of an incipient Amazon who wore a Blazer and walked like a Policeman.

She did not hamper her fibrous Physique with any excess Harness that might pinch when she essayed a full St. Andrew's Swipe with a wooden Club. And she had one lower octave of Pipes, like a Brakeman on the Erie.

There comes a brief Period in the Veal Epoch of every Sentimental Tommy when the only real Cutie is one who can propel a Canoe and throw Overhand.

So Walter, such being the baptismal Handicap, often thought it would be Sweet Billiards to keep house with the she-Acrobat for 30 or 40 years, because when they were tired of sitting in the House they could go into the Front Yard and play Ketch.

He was just at the rickety Age when the Gams refuse to co-ordinate. Every time he sauntered carelessly across the porch at a Summer Hotel, he gave a correct Imitation of a troop of Cavalry going over a Wooden Bridge at full Gallop.

He had a way of backing into Potted Plants.

Each Morning was clouded by the task of picking out a Cravat that would be of the same Radio-Activity as his Socks. And all through the waking hours he carried with him a faint and sickly Realization that his Parents did not understand him.

One day he stood before a kind-faced Registrar and matriculated. Branded as a regular Freshman, he went back to his little Den and put a news-stand Photo of Lillian Russell between two Pennants.

The whalebone Divinity in the Home Town passed out of his Life. He told himself that he would be true to Miss Russell and all the other Members of her sprightly Profession.

The emotional side of his unfolding Nature began to nourish itself on Song Hits, and he slept each night with his Banjo folded tightly to his Bosom.

He became acquainted with a Sophomore who once sat near Trixie Friganza in a Parlor Car. One night Alice Nielsen looked directly at the Box in which he was seated with the other Fraters of the Ippy Ki Yi. In fact, his Life became crowded with tingling Experiences.

The collection of Cigarette Pictures made him acquainted with many Celebrities. His intimacy with them grew apace as he developed a bookish appetite for Sunday Newspapers.

He danced with the local Chickadees, but all the time his Heart was far away, in the Dramatic Column.

Suddenly he found that he was an Upper Classman, to whom each Neophyte touched the Leaf of Lettuce balanced on top of the Head, ostensibly as a Cap.

He became endowed with the divine Right to hit himself on the Leg with a Walking Stick and sit on a hallowed Fence.

Simultaneous-like, he became conscious of the fact that the Footlight Favorites were no longer worthy of him. He began to hold long and serious Conversaziones with the Sister of a Prof.

She was an aerial Performer who wore powerful Spectacles, in which any one standing before her could see an Image of himself, greatly reduced. She looked as if she had been sitting up all night, writing a History of Civilization.

Walter found himself uplifted every time they were left together in the Library. Sometimes she took him up so high that he became dizzy.

He now began to prog as follows: He and the Lady Emerson would be legally welded just after Commencement and spend the Honeymoon at some lively Chautauqua.

The grinding Wheels and raucous buying and selling of the Marts of Trade seemed faint and far away when he roamed through the Cloisters with Elfreda. He was in the moulting Stage, and it seemed to him that Success in Life would consist of going about reeking of Culture.

A Degree looked bigger than a Dividend.

He never had heard tell of such a thing as a Coal-Bill or a Special Assessment for a Sewer.

The vision of Elfreda floated out through a Transom three days after he drew a Desk in the extensive Works owned by the Governor.

He was too busy keeping his Head above the Churning Waves to bother with Speculative Philosophy or write Letters studded with Latin Phrases, like Currants in an English Cake.

All the cringing Peons in the big Stockade hated him because he had a Drag. It was up to him to deliver the Merchandise and demonstrate that he was a Human Being rather than a College Graduate.

In the meantime, the Spectators were hoping that he would Skid and go into the Fence.

He began to wear his Frat pin on his undershirt, and he had no time to frivol away on the fluffy Gender, because he expected to be sitting in the Directors' Room in a couple of years, talking it over with Henry C. Frick.

So he waved aside the Square Envelopes and allowed himself to be billed all over the Macaroon Circuit as a Woman-Hater.

Of course he girled in a conservative way, but he merely trailed. He did not buzz, or throw himself at the fallen

Handkerchief, or run to get the Wraps, or do any of the Stuff that marks the true and bounden Captive.

When he found himself in the cushioned Lair of a Feline, he would lean back in perfect Security, knowing that even if she exercised her entire repertoire of Wiles, she could not warm the Dead Heart nor stir into life the fallen Rose Leaves of Romance.

All the time she was spilling her familiar line of Chatter, he would look at her with an arid and patronizing Smile, such as the Harvard Man produces when he finds himself in immediate juxtaposition to some human Caterpillar from west of Pittsburgh.

Very often, when the registered Dolly Grays got together for a Bon-Bon Orgy, some one would say, "Oh, Crickey, ain't he the regular Cynic?" Another might suggest that he was hiding a great Sorrow, his whole Existence having been embittered by the faithlessness of some Creature. Then they would take a Vote and decide that he was a plain Mutt.

The Chauncey who refuses to reciprocate will excite more Conversation than a regular Union Lover, but it is Lucky for him that he does not hear all the Conversation.

Walter at the age of twenty-five thought he was too old and sedate to be a Diner-Out and Dancing Devil.

When he was 28, however, he had become Hep to the large and luminous Truth that the man who sits in his Lodgings reading Dumas may overlook many a Bet.

He noted on every Hand the nice-looking Boys who turned in about 10.40 and avoided the Pitfalls of Society, and most of them were pulling down as much as $14 a week.

He recalled what this humble Chronicler had said away back in 1899: "Early to Bed and Early to Rise and you will meet very few of our Best People."

He looked over the Lay-Out and decided that it was just as easy to mingle with the Face Cards as to sleep in the Discards.

He saw many a Light Weight with a gilt sign exposed on Main Street and no Assets except a Suit with a Velvet Collar, a pair of indestructible dancing Legs, and just enough intellectual Acumen to stir Tea without spilling it.

So he decided to have a try at the Gay Life and worm his way into the Safety Deposit Vaults via the Parlor Route.

A worthy Resolve and one often taken.

If a Friend of the People can capitalize his Vocal Cords, why should not the little Brother of the Rich put his undying Nerve into the Market and get what he can on it?

The Captain of Finance is usually owned, Body and Soul, by the other Half of the Sketch. She may be a head bell-ringer in the D. A. R. or the blue-pencil Queen of the Golden Pheasants, but in a vast majority of cases she has not the Looks to back up the Title.

Even the Buckingham Palace manner and the Arctic Front cannot buffalo the idle Spectator into overlooking the fact that she belongs to the genus Quince.

She may not be a Beaut, but it is She who stands at the main entrance to the Big Tent and tears off seat coupons.

Walter knew that if he wished to be mentioned all over town as a Sure-Enough, his passport to the Inner Circle of Hot Potatoes would have to be vised by Patroness No. 1.

He began to work in the Secret Service of the Chosen Few and was First Aid to the Chaperons.

A Hard Life, say you? Not a tall—not a tall.

He was entirely surrounded by Fairy Lamps and sweet-smelling Flowers. Life became a kaleidoscopic Aurora Borealis.

When the first Crash of Music came through the hothouse Palms, Walter would be out on the Waxen Floor with his hair in a Braid.

Through the long watches of the night he played Blonde against Brunette and then went home with his Time-Card bearing the official O. K..

He swam among the floating Hooks and side-stepped the Maternal Traps, until the compilers of Marital Statistics had his name in the list marked "Nothing Doing."

The Dope on him seemed to be that he was Immune and Jinx-Proof.

After he led one of them back to a Divan and fed her an Ice it was a case of "Good Night, Miss Mitchell."

Truly, a Bachelor flown with Insolence and Pride is the favorite Mark for the Bow-and-Arrow Kid. For every weather-beaten Beau and Ballroom Veteran there is waiting somewhere in Ambuscade a keen little Diana with the right kind of Ammunition.

One night he went to a Small Dance in his regular Henry Miller suit and wearing a tired look around the Eyes. He counted these minor Functions a dreadful Bore.

Over in a corner sat a half-portion Damosel who had come to town on aVisit. Her name was Violet, and she looked the Part.

She didn't know who was running for President or what Miss Pankhurst said about Suffrage, but she had large belladonna Orbs, with Danger lurking in their limpid depths.

She was just at the Age when any girl who is not actually Deformed looks fair to middling, while the real Dinger, with the Tresses and the Complexion and the gleaming white Shoulders and the Parisian figure, is right there with a full equipment for breaking up Families.

Old Dare-Devil Dick, the Hero of 1000 Flirtations, was sitting out one of the Dances recently condemned by Press and Pulpit.

He became aware of the presence of something Feminine at his immediate right. He took a cautious Look and beheld a timid Debutante, sparkling with the Dew and waiting to be plucked.

She gave him a frightened Smile and lamped him very slowly.

Suddenly he felt himself wafted away on a cloud of Purple Perfumery. She had put the Sign on him without lifting a Finger.

His friends tried to save him. They demonstrated, with a Pencil and a Piece of Paper, that she was just an ordinary, everyday Baby Doll with a Second Reader intelligence and the Spiritual Caliber of a Humming Bird. They proved that exactly the same kind were scattered through every Department Store, working for $6 a week.

When they got thorough knocking, he hurried over and told her everything and promised her that if she would marry him, not one of these Snakes would ever be permitted to enter the House.

He writhed on the Rug and said that if she didn't whisper that One Little Word, it would be a case of Satin Lining and Silver Handles for little Wallie.

She looked out the Window and yawned slightly and then said, "Oh, very well."

He rode home standing up in a Taxicab, while she was showing the Maids a lozenge-shaped Ring that set him back 450 Bucks.

MORAL: The higher they fly the harder they fall.

THE NEW FABLE OF THE SEARCH FOR CLIMATE

Once there was a Gentleman of the deepest dye who was all out of Kilter. He felt like a list of Symptoms on the outside of a Dollar Bottle. He looked like the Picture you see in the Almanac entitled, "Before Taking."

When his Liver was at Perihelion, he had a Complexion suggesting an Alligator-Pear, and his Eye-Balls should have been taken out and burnished.

He could see little dirigible Balloons drifting about in all parts of the deep-blue Ether. His Tummy told him that some one had moved in and was giving a Chafing-Dish Party. Furthermore, a red-hot Awl had been inserted under each Shoulder Blade.

When every Tree was a Weeping Willow and the Sun went slinking behind a Cloud, his only definite Yearn was to crawl into a dark Cellar with Fungus on the Walls and do the Shuffle, after making a sarcastic Will that disinherited all Relatives and Friends.

This poor, stricken Gloomer had time-tabled himself all over the Universe, trying to close in on a Climate that would put him on his Feet and keep him Fit as a Fiddle.

He had de-luxed himself to remote Spots that were supplied with Steam Heat and French Cooking, together with Wines, Liquors, and Cigars, but no matter what the Altitude or the

Relative Humidity, he felt discouraged every Morning when he awoke and remembered that presently he would have to rally his Vital Forces and walk all the way to the Tub.

It was too bad that a Clubman, so eminent Socially, should be thus shot to Rags and Fragments. Could aught be more Piteous than to Witness a proud and haughty Income tottering along the Street, searching in vain for a Workingman's Appetite? When one with a spending possibility of $2 a Minute is told by a Specialist to drink plenty of Hot Water, the Words seem almost Ironic.

His Operating Expenses kept running up, and yet it looked like sheer Waste to lavish so much Collateral on the upkeep of a Physical Swab.

To show you how he worked at recouping his Health, once he spent a whole Summer in Merrie England. He had been told by a Globe-Trotter that One lodging within a mile of Trafalgar Square could hoist unlimited Scotch and yet sidestep the Day After.

The Explanation offered by members of the Royal Alcoholic Society is that the Moisture in the Atmosphere counter-balances or nullifies, so to speak, the interior Wetness.

Also, the normal state of Melancholy is such that even a case of Katzenjammer merely blends in with the surrounding Drabness.

He experimented sincerely with the Caledonian Cure, acquiring a rich sunset Glow, much affected by half-pay Majors and the elderly Toffs who ride in the Row. He began to wear his Arteries on the outside, just like a true son of Albion. This cherry-ripe Facial Tint proves that the Britisher is the most rugged Chap in the World—except when he is in Stockholm.

In fact, if the New York Duds worn by the Yank had been less of a Fit, and he could have schooled himself to look at a Herring without shuddering, he might have rung in as a Resident of the tight little Isle, for he was often Tight.

He learned to like the Smoky Taste and could even take it warm, but still he felt Rocky, and up to 3 P. M. was only about 30 per cent. Human.

One evening in a polite Pub he heard about the wonderful Vin Ordinaire of Sunny France. He was told that the Peasants who irrigated themselves with a brunette Fluid resembling diluted Ink were husky as Beeves and simply staggering with Health.

So he went motoring in the Grape and Chateau District and played Claret both ways from the Middle. Every time the Petrol chariot pulled up in front of a Brasserie, he would call for a Flagon of some rare old Vintage squeezed out the day before.

Then he would go riding at the rate of 82 Kilos an Hour, scooping up the Climate as he scooted along.

Notwithstanding all these brave Efforts to overtake Health, he would feel like a frost-nipped Rutabaga when the matutinal Chanticleer told him that another blue Dawn was sneaking over the Hills.

He began to figure himself a Candidate for a plain white Cot in the Nerve Garage, when he heard of the wonderful Air and Dietary Advantages of Germany. It seemed that the Fatherland was becoming Commercially Supreme and of the greatest Military Importance because every Fritz kept himself saturated with the Essence of Munich.

He could see on the Post-Cards that each loyal subject of Wilhelm was plump and rosy, with Apple Cheeks and a well-defined Awning just below the Floating Ribs, and a Krug of dark Suds clutched in the right Mitt.

All the way from Duesseldorf to Wohlgebaum he played the Circuit of Gardens with nice clean Gravel on the Ground and Dill Pickles festooned among the Caraway Trees. Every time the Military Band began to breathe a new Waltz he would have Otto bring a Tub of the Dark Brew and a Frankfurter about the size of a Sash Weight.

Between pulls he would suspire deeply, so as to get the full assistance of the Climate.

Sometimes he would feel that he was being benefitted.

Often at 9 P. M., before taking his final Schnitzel and passing gently into a state of Coma, he would get ready to renounce allegiance to all three of the Political Parties in the U. S. A. and grow one of those U-Shaped Mustaches.

Next Morning, like as not, he would emerge from beneath the Feather Tick and lean against the Porcelain Stove, wondering vaguely if he could live through the Day.

The very Treatment which developed large and coarse-grained Soldiers all through Schleswig-Holstein seemed to make this Son of Connecticut just about as gimpy as a wet Towel.

Undismayed by repeated Failures, he took some Advice, given in a Rathskeller, and went to a Mountain Resort famous for a certain brand of White Vinegar with a colored Landscape on the Label.

It was said that anyone becoming thoroughly acidulated with this noble Beverage would put a Feather into his Granulated Lid and begin to Yodel.

He sat among the snowy Peaks, entirely surrounded by the rarefied Atmosphere so highly boosted in the Hotel Circulars, sampling a tall bottle of every kind ending with "heimer," and yet he didn't seem to get the Results.

George Ade

At last he headed for the barbaric Region which an unkindly Fate had designated as Home, almost convinced that there was no Climate on the Map which would really adapt itself to all the intricate Peculiarities of his complicated Case.

Often he would be found in the Reception Room just next to the shake-down Parlor.

After reading a few pages in a popular Magazine dated two Years back, he would be admitted to the little inside Room, faintly perfumed with something other than New Mown Hay. Here he would cower before the dollar-a-minute Specialist, who would apply a Dictograph to the Heart Region and then say "You are all Run Down."

Next day the Sufferer would collect his folding Trunks and Head-Ache Tablets and Hot-Water Bags and start for Florida or California or the Piney Woods.

Sometimes he would seem to perk up for a Day or two. Enlivened by Hopeand a few Dry Martinis, he would move up to a little Table in the shade of the sheltering Candelabrum and tackle the Carte du Jour from Caviar to Cafe Noir.

The Climate would seem to be helping his Appetite.

Within 24 Hours, however, he would be craving only some cold Carbonic and a few Kind Words.

Florida seemed to enervate him. California was too unsettled. Even in the Mountains, his Heart always bothered him after a Hearty Meal. And the Piney Woods only made him Pine more than ever.

Time and again he would curl up in the palatial Drawing-Room at one end of the Sleeper and dream that six Life-Long Friends in deep Black were whispering among the Floral Tributes and putting on Cotton Gloves.

While searching for the Fountain of Youth he would bump into Sympathetic Souls of the kind who infest Observation Cars and hold down Rocking-Chairs in front of Wooden Hotels. These Fellow Voyagers in the realm of Hypochondria would give him various Capsules and Tablets, supposed to be good for whatever Ailed one at the Time. So eager was he to regain his full vigor and be able to eat and drink everything forbidden by the Doctors, he would fall for every kind of Dope made from Coal Tar.

Even if he had worn Blinders he could not have walked past an Apothecary Shop.

As he moved about the produced a muffled Castanet Effect, for he had a little box of Medicated Bullets in every Pocket.

Yet he was not in Condition.

His Complexion was a Bird's-Eye Maple, and he looked like the Superintendent of a prosperous Morgue.

One Summer Day, when he was only about three jumps ahead of a Cataleptic Convulsion, he had to get on the Cars and take a long ride to inspect some Copper Mines which helped to fatten his impotent Income. The train was bowling through a placid Dairy Region in the Commonwealth regulated by Mr. La Follette.

The Chronic Invalid was in the Buffet, trying to work up a Desire for Luncheon, when suddenly the Car turned a complete Somersault, because a heavy Freight Train had met Number Six head on.

When the Subject of this Treatise came to, he was propped up on the front porch of a Farm House with one Leg in Splits and a kind-faced Lady pressing Cold Applications to the fevered Brow.

He was O. K. except that he would have to lie still for a few

Weeks while the Bones did their Knitting.

The good Country Folk would not permit him to be moved. He was dead willing to sink back among the White Pillows and figure the Accident Insurance.

Through the Honeysuckles and Morning-Glories he could see the long slope of the Clover Pasture, with here and there a deliberate Cow, and the Steeple of the Reformed Church showing above a distant clump of Soft Maples.

About two hours after emerging from the trance, he made his customary Diagnosis and discovered that he was nervously shattered and in urgent need of a most heroic Bracer. He beckoned to the president of the local W. C. T. U. and said if they were all out of Scotch, he could do with a full-sized Hooker of any standard Bourbon that had matured in the Wood and was not blended.

Nurse readjusted his Pillow and told him that as soon as he came out of the Delirium he could dally with a mug of Buttermilk.

By and by, as he gathered Strength, she would slip him some Weak Tea.

He had heard that in some of these outlying Regions, the Family Sideboard stood for nothing stronger than Mustard, but this was the first time he had met Human Beings who were not on visiting Terms with the Demon Rum.

At the Cocktail Hour he ventured a second Request for any one of the standard Necessities of Life, but Mrs. Peabody read him a Passage from the Family Medicine Book to the effect that Liquor was never to be used except for Snake Bites.

When he ordered the Hired Hand to bring him a large Snake, they gave him a Sleeping Powder and told inquiring Neighbors that he was still out of his Head.

Next day he found himself alive, thanks to a wonderful Constitution. The Samaritans came and stood around his Couch and jollied him and offered him everything except what he needed.

When he offered to compromise on Drug-Store Sherry, the Daughter of theHousehold, Luella by name, brought out a colored Chart showing the Interior of a Moderate Drinker's Stomach. After that he was afraid to Chirp.

Even the Cigarette was Taboo among these Good People, although Father could Fletcherize about 10 cents' worth of Licorice Plug each working Day.

Far removed from the Lad with the White Apron, and with nothing to inhale except Ozone, the unhappy Bon Vivant was compelled to put up with these most unnatural Conditions.

When he was tired of dozing he could take his choice of any kind of Milk and read a few more pages of Robinson Crusoe.

Then ensued the Miracle.

His Nerves began to unspiral themselves and lie down. He began to sit up and listen for the Toot of the Dinner Horn.

As soon as he could hobble on Crutches they put him on the Hay Scales, and he thought the Thing was out of Whack, for he had taken on 4 Pounds.

The Fresh Garden truck seemed superior to any that he had been able to obtain in the Best Restaurants.

What was more amazing, he now evinced a critical Interest in Clydesdale Colts and Leghorn Roosters, although nothing of the sort had ever come into his Life while he had an Apartment in Forty-seventh Street.

When he took his game Leg back to the Metropolis, he hurried

George Ade

to the Club and made a startling Report to all the broken-down Sports assembled in the Card-Room.

He said he had discovered the only Climate in the World. It had Switzerland skinned and was not enervating, like Florida, for he had been sleeping like a Baby and felt like a 2-year-old every A. M., in spite of the fact that he could not get his regular Rations.

He wanted to organize a Company and build a Million Dollar Hotel at Once.

With a New York Steward to supply the Table and a well-stocked Cellar, the Resort ought to get all the classy Trade, for he hoped to die if the Air out there hadn't done more for him in One Month than Europe had done in the whole Year.

MORAL: Nature will sometimes help the Unfortunate who finds it impossible to reach out and help Himself.

THE NEW FABLE OF THE FATHER WHO JUMPED IN

Once there was a leading Citizen with only one Daughter, but she was Some Offspring.

Bernice was chief Expense Account and Crown Jewel of a Real Estate Juggler who had done so well that all the Strap-Hangers regarded him as an Enemy to Society.

Papa was foolish, even as a Weasel.

He was what you might call Honest, which signified that all of his Low Work had been done by Agents.

A Person of rare judgment, withal. He never copped a piece of bulky Swag unless he had a Wheelbarrow with him at the time.

He had been going East with the Green Goods ever since the Party in Power precipitated the first Panic.

He had Stacks of the Needful, and his Rating was AA Plus 1, to say nothing of a Reserve cached in the little Tin Box.

Daughter alone could include him to unbuckle, and melt, and jar loose, and come across, and kick in, and sting the Check-Book.

One day Bernice was a Little Girl, and the next she was head Flossie among the Debutantes, with a pack of Society Hounds pursuing in Full Cry, each willing to help count the Bank Roll.

Father was scared pink when he sized up the Field.

He still wore box-toed Boots and carried Foliage on the Sub-Maxillary so that those who came ringing the Front Bell didn't look very lucky to him.

Sometimes he would dream that he had been pushed into a Mausoleum and that a slender Cyril with a Lady's Watch strapped on his wrist was spending all of that Money for Signed Etchings.

Whereupon he would awake in a Cold Sweat and try to think of a safe Recipe for poisoning Boulevard Blighters.

One day Bernice went out into the Sunshine and found something and brought it home with her and put it on a Rug in the Elizabethan Room.

Father came in and took one look and said: "Not for Mine! I won't stand for any Puss Willow being grafted on to our Family Tree."

His name was Kenneth, and he reduced his Percentage on the first day by having the hem-stitched Mouchoir tucked inside of the Cuff.

Also, it was rumored that he put oil on his Eye-Brows and rubbed Perfumery on the backs of his Hands.

Father walked around the He-Canary twice, looking at him over the Specs, and then he rushed to the Library and kicked the Upholstery out of an $80 chair.

He could see the love-light glinting in the Eyes of Bernice. She had fallen for the Flukus.

Kenneth was installed as Steady.

When Bernice saw him turn the Corner and approach the House, he looked to her like Rupert, the long lost Heir—while Father discerned only an insect too large to be treated with Powder.

Kenneth was the kind of Sop that you see wearing Evening Clothes on a Colored Post-Card.

If his private Estate had been converted into Pig Iron, he could have carried it in his Watch Pocket.

He was re-fined and had lovely Teeth, but those who knew him well believed the Story that when he was a Babe in Arms, the Nurse had let him fall and strike on the Head.

He wore his Hair straight back and used Patent Leather dressing. He was full of Swank and put on much Side and wore lily-colored Spats and was an awful Thing all around, from Pa's point of view.

In a crowd of Bank Directors he would have been a cheap Swivel, but among the Women Folks he was a regular Bright Eyes.

When you passed through the Archway of his Intellectual Domain you found yourself in the Next Block.

But—he could go into a Parlor and sprinkle Soothing Syrup all over the Rugs.

He had a Vaudeville Education and a small Tenor Voice, with the result that many a fluttering Birdie regarded him as the bona-fide Ketchup. Bernice thought she was lucky to have snared him away from the others, and she had slipped him the whispered Promise, come Weal, come Woe. She had no Mother to guide her, and it looked as if the Family was about to have a Bermuda wished on to it.

No wonder Father was stepping sideways.

He would come home in the evening and find the Mush perched on a Throne in the Spot Light, shooting an azure-blue Line of desiccated Drool, with Bernice sitting out in front and Encoring.

Then he would retire to the back part of the House to bark at the Butler and act as if he had been eating Red Meat.

He knew that if he elbowed in and tried to break up the Clinch, it would mean a Rope Ladder, a piece in the Papers, and a final Reconciliation, with Parent playing the usual role of Goat.

He was resolved not to put in the remainder of his Days being panhandled by a Souffle who wore Dancing Pumps in the Daytime. The problem was to get shut of the Rodent without resorting to any Rough Stuff.

Father had never heard tell of the Perils of Propinquity, and he thought Psychology had something to do with Fish.

Just the same, he remembered about a Quail a day for 30 days, and he knew that the most agreeable Perfumery would not smell right if applied with a Garden Hose.

Likewise, he suspected that many a Quarter-Horse would blow, if put into a two-mile Handicap.

So he blocked out a Program which proved that Solomon had nothing on him.

Instead of grilling young Kenneth and holding him up to Contumely and forbidding him the use of the Cozy Corner, he started in to boost the Love Match.

Kenneth all but moved in his Trunk.

Father had a chance to weigh him, down to the last Ounce, and study the simple Mechanism of his transparent Personality.

Father classified the would-be Child-in-Law as a Gobbie, which means a Home-Wrecker who is still learning his Trade.

The Candidate became a regular Boarder.

Kenneth would sit right up close to old Cash-in-Hand, who would egg him on to tell Dialect Stories and, after that, show how to make a Salad. The Stories were some that Marshall Wilder stopped using in 1882 and since then have been outlawed on the Kerosene Circuit.

After Bernice had heard these Almanac Wheezes 26 or 28 times, she would sit still and look at the Center-Piece while Lover was performing.

The Gags didn't sound as killing as they had at first, and sometimes she wished the Dear Boy would chop on them.

No chance. Father had him kidded into believing that all the old ham-fat Riddles were simply Immense.

As for that Salad Specialty, the poor Gink who calls loudly for English Mustard and thinks he is a Genius because he can rub a Bowl with a sprig of Garlic, may have his brief Hour of Triumph, but no man ever really got anywhere by doping Salad, when you stop to add it all up.

Father would put the two young people together in the back of the Touring Car and ride them around for Hours at a time.

Anybody who has cut in on one of those animated Automobile Conversations, while the salaried Maniac from France is hitting up 42 miles an Hour, will tell you that the hind end of a Motor Vehicle is no good Trysting Place for an Engaged Couple.

Bernice would get home after one of these wild swoops into the realm of the Death Angel, and totter to her room and lie down, and murmur: "I wonder what ailed Kenneth to-day. He seemed Preoccupied."

That Same Evening, just when she needed Smelling Salts and Absolute Quiet, her enthusiastic Father would have Fiance up to Dinner and pull the same stale Repertoire and splash around in the Oil and Vinegar.

If any Guests were present, then Father would play Introducer and tell them beforehand how good Kenneth was.

When given his Cue, the Lad would swell up and spring a hot One about the Swede and the Irishman, while Bernice would fuss with the Salt and wonder dimly if the Future had aught in store for her except Dialect Stuff.

Father had read on a Blotter somewhere that Absence makes the Heart grow fonder, so he played his System with the Reverse English. He arranged a nice long trip by Land and Water and took the male Sweetheart along, so that the Doting Pair could be together at Breakfast.

His cunning had now become diabolical. He was getting ready to apply the Supreme Test.

Every Morning, when Bernice looked over her Baked Apple she saw nothing in this wide World except Kenneth, still reeking of Witch Hazel and spotted with Talcum Powder, and not very long on Sparkling Conversation.

When he was propped up in the cold Dawn, with his eyes partially open, he did not resemble a Royal Personage nearly as much as he had in some of his earlier Photographs.

Father would order soft-boiled Eggs to be Eaten from the Shell. When Kenneth got around to these, he would cease to be a Romantic Figure for at least a few Minutes. Bernice would turn away in dread and look out at the swaying Trees and long to see some of her Girl Friends back home.

After Kenneth had been served to her, three meals a day, for two Weeks and they had ridden together for Ages and Ages, in Pullman Compartments, she made certain horrible Discoveries.

One of his Ears was larger than the other.

He made a funny noise with his Adam's Apple when drinking Hot Coffee.

When he was annoyed, he bit his nails.

When suffering from a Cold, he was Sniffy.

The first time she became aware of the slight discrepancy in Ears, she suffered only a slight Annoyance. It handed her a tiny Pang to find a Flaw in a Piece of Work that she had regarded as Perfect.

After she had seen nothing else but those Ears for many, many Days, it became evident to her that if Kenneth truly loved her, he would go and have them fixed.

Likewise, every time her Heart's Delight lifted the Cup to his Ruby Lips, she would grip the Table Cloth with both Hands, and whisper to herself, "Now we get the Funny Noise."

Kenneth, in the mean while, had found out that her Hair did not always look the same, but one who is striving to get a Meal Ticket for Life cannot be over-fastidious.

He was Game and stood ready to obey all Orders in order to pull down the Capital Prize.

He had been such a Hit in the Maple-Sundae Set that he could not conceive the possibility of any Female becoming satiated with his Society.

The poor Loon never stopped to figure out that the only way

to keep a Girl sitting up and interested is to stay away once in a while and give her a Vacation.

Father was right on the Job to see that Bernice had no Vacation. He framed it up to give her a Foretaste of Matrimony every Day in the Week. If the Future Husband wandered more than thirty feet from her side, Father would nail him and Sic him on to her again.

She would look up and say: "Oh, Fury! Look who's here again!"

This was no way for a true-hearted Maiden to speak of her Soul Mate.

Father put the Cap Sheaf on his big Experiment by accepting an invitation to go Yachting.

He put them side by side on Deck and told them to comfort each other, in case anything happened.

They never could have been quite the same to each other after that Day. Bernice wanted to get back on Shore and hunt her Room and peel down to a Kimono and refuse any Callers for a Month.

Even the accepted Swain was beginning to slow up. He could remember the time when he used to sit around with members of his own Sex.

Father had no Mercy. He took the two Invalids back to Land and rounded them up for Breakfast next morning.

When Kenneth appeared, he was slightly greenish in Color.

One Ear was three times as large as the other. He had caught a Sniffy Cold.

In partaking of his Coffee he made Sounds similar to those

coming through the Partition when the People in the adjoining Flat have trouble with the Plumbing.

He saw Bernice glaring at him and bit his Nails in Embarrassment.

Father felt the Crisis impending and laid on the last Straw.

"I was trying to recall that Story," said he—"the One about the German and the Dog."

Bernice gave one Shriek and then dashed from the Room, making hysterical Outcries along the Corridor.

Father told Kenneth to check all the Trunks for Home and then catch an early Train.

Bernice was squirming about on the Hotel Sofa when Father entered the Room.

She threw herself into his Arms and passionately demanded, "Why, oh, why are you trying to force me into marrying that Creature?"

MORAL: Don't get acquainted too soon.

THE NEW FABLE OF THE UPLIFTER
AND HIS DANDY LITTLE OPUS

Once there was a Litry Guy who would don his Undertaker's Regalia and the White Satin Puff Tie and go out of an Afternoon to read a Paper to the Wimmen.

At every Tea Battle and Cookie Carnival he was hailed as the Big Hero. A good many pulsating Dulcineas who didn't know what "Iconoclast" meant, regarded him as an awful Iconoclast.

And cynical? Mercy!

When he stood up in a Front Room and Unfolded his MS., and swallowed the Peppermint Wafer and began to Bleat, no one in the World of Letters was safe.

He would wallop Dickens and jounce Kipling and even take a side-swipe at Luella Prentiss Budd, who was the Poetess Laureate for the Ward in which he lived.

Ever since his Stuff had been shot back by a Boston Editor with a Complimentary Note, he had billed himself as an Author and had been pointed out as such at more than one Chautauqua.

Consequently his Views on Recent Fiction carried much weight with the Carries.

He loved to pile the Fagots around a Best Seller and burn it to a Cinder, while the Girls past 30 years of Age sat in front of him and Shuddered.

As for the Drama, he could spread a New York Success on the marble-top Table and dissect it until nothing was left but the Motif, and then he would heave that into the Waste Basket, thereby leaving the Stage in America flat on its back.

And if you mentioned Georgie Cohan to him, the Foam would begin to fleck his Lips and he would go plumb Locoed.

After he had been sitting on the Fence for many years, booing those who tried to saw Wood, his Satellites began coaxing him to write something that would show up Charley Klein and Gus Thomas and all the other Four-Flushers who were raking in Royalties under False Pretences.

They knew he was a Genius, because nothing pleased him.

He decided to start with something easy and dash off an Operetta. Having sat through some of the Current Offerings, he noted that the Dialogue was unrelated to Real Literature and the Verses lacked Metrical Symmetry.

It would be a Pipe for a sure-enough Bard to sit down on a Rainy Afternoon and grind out something that might serve as a Model for Harry B. Smith.

So he had a Vase of Fresh Flowers put on his Desk every Day, and he would sit there, waiting for the Muse to keep her Date.

At the end of a Month he had it all planned to lay the First Scene in front of a Palace with a Forest on the Back Drop so as to get a lot of Atmosphere.

There was to be a Princess in the Thing, and a Picture of the long-lost Mother in the Locket and other New Stuff.

He put in Hours and Hours hand-embroidering the Verses.

When he made "Society" rhyme with "Propriety," he thought he was getting Gilbertian.

While these Lyrics were still quivering, he would take them out and read them to his wife and the Hired Girl and the man who attended to the Furnace, and get their Impartial Judgement.

They agreed that it was Hot Gravy and too good for the Stage.

Encouraged by these heart-felt Encomiums, he would hike back to the Study, shoot himself in the Arm with a hypothetical Needle, and once more begin picking Grapes in Arcady.

When People came to the House, not knowing that he had been taken down with anything, he would own up that he was working on a Mere Trifle, and then, after being sufficiently urged, he would give a Reading.

These Readings could have been headed off only by an Order of Court or calling out the State Guard.

Inasmuch as the large-size Carnegie Medal for Heroism is waiting for the Caller who has the immortal Rind to tell a poetical Pest that his output is Punk, the Author found himself smeared with Compliments after each of these parlor Try-Outs.

They kidded him into thinking that he had incubated a Whale.

When he had chewed up a Gross of Pencils and taken enough Tea to float the Imperator, the great Work was complete and ready to be launched with a loud Splash.

He began to inquire the Name of some prominent Theatre Blokie who was a keen Student of the Classics and a Person of super-refined Taste. The man he sought had moved into the Poor House, so he compromised by expressing his typewritten Masterpiece to a Ringmaster whose name he had seen on the

Three Sheets. It was marked, "Valuable Package." In a few months the hirelings of the Company and the Driver of the Wagon became well acquainted with the Large Envelope containing the only Hope of the present decadent Period.

Every time the Work came back to him, with a brief printed Suggestion that any Male Adult not physically disabled could make $1.75 a day with a Shovel, the Author would appear at the Afternoon Club with another scathing arraignment of certain Commercial Aspects of the Modern Stage. He saw that it was over their Heads.

It was too darned Dainty for a Flat-Head who spelt Art with a lower-case "a."

Yet it was so drenched and saturated and surcharged with Merit that he resolved to have it done by Local Amateurs rather than see it lost to the World.

The Music was written by Genius No. 2, working in a Piano Store. He had been writing Great Music for years.

Whenever he heard something catchy, he went home and wrote it.

He was very Temperamental. That is, he got soused on about three, and, while snooted, would deride Victor Herbert, thus proving that he was Brilliant, though Erratic.

He had a trunkful of Tunes that were too scholarly for the Ikeys who publish Popular Trash.

He fitted them on to the Libretto written by the Litry Guy.

When the two got together to run over the Book and Score, they were sure enthusiastic.

The Author said the Lines were the best he had ever heard, and the Composer said the Numbers were all Gems.

When the Home Talent bunch pulled the whole Affair before a mob of Personal Friends and a subsidized City Editor, it was a Night of Triumph for all concerned.

The trained and trusty Liars who, in every Community, wear Evening Clothes and stand around at Receptions, all crowded up to the Author and gave him the Cordial Mitt and boosted something scandalous. He didn't know that all of them Knocked after they got around the Dutch Lunch.

He went home, sobbing with Joy. That night he nominated himself for the Hall of Fame and put it to a Vote, and there was not one Dissenting Voice.

Every deluded Boob who can bat up Fungoes in his own Back Yard thinks he is qualified to break into a Major League and line out Two-Baggers.

There was no holding the inspired Librettist and the talented young Composer.

They knew that the eager Public in 48 States was waiting for the Best Thing since "Robin Hood."

The Author went up to the City and found a Manager who had a Desk and a lot of Courage and a varied experience in risking other people's Coin. After the two Geniuses had mortgaged their Homes, the Impresario was enabled to get some Scenery built and rally a large Drove of Artists—most of them carrying Hand Bags.

During Rehearsals the brutal Stage Manager wanted to cut the Gizzard out of the Book and omit most of the sentimental Arias, but Mr. Words and Mr. Music emitted such shrieks of protest against the threatened Sacrilege that he allowed all the select home-made Guff to remain in the Script.

He thought it would serve them right.

When they gave the first Real Performance in a Dog Town on a drizzly evening in November, there was not Social Eclat to fill the sails.

The House was mostly Paper and therefore very Missouri.

Also a full delegation from the Coffin-Trimmers' Union with Cracked Ice in their Laps.

They did not owe any Money to the Author or have any Kinfolk in the Cast, so they sat back with their Hands under them and allowed the pretty little Opera to die like an Outcast.

The only Laugh in the Piece was when the Drop Curtain refused to work.

After the Show the Manager met them at an Oyster House and told them they had eased a Persimmon to him.

He said the whole Trick was a Bloomer. It was just as funny as a Wooden Leg. It needed much Pep and about two tons of Bokum.

Both Words and Music refused to countenance any radical Changes. They said it would be another "Cavalleria" as soon as they could do it before an intelligent Audience of True-Lovers.

The Ex-Minstrel Man said there wasn't no such Animal as an intelligent Play-goer.

The Simp that pushed his Metal into the Box Office wanted Something Doing every minute and many Gals, otherwise it was back to the Store-House and a Card in the Clipper.

The Call on the Board read "Everybody at Ten," but the brainy Writer and the versatile Composer were not included.

When they appeared at the Stage Door they were met by Props, who told them to get to a certain Place out of there.

Standing in the Alley, they could hear Wails of Anguish, and they knew that their Child was having the Vital Organs removed.

The celebrated Author of the Graveyard Rag had been summoned in haste. He was in charge of the Clinic—taking out the Grammar and putting in Gags.

The Duos and Ensembles were being dropped through the Trap Door to make way for recent Song Hits from the alcoholic Cabarets.

The Ax fell right on the powdered Neck of the beautiful Prima Donna, who had studied for Grand Opera, but never had been able to find an Orchestra that would fit her Voice.

Her Part was changed from a Princess to a Shop-Lifter and was assigned to Cissy St. Vitus, late of a Burlesque Bunch known as the Lady Bugs. The Tenor was given the Hook, and his sentimental Role was entrusted to a Head-Spinner who had acquired his Dramatic Schooling with the Ringling Circus.

All of which comes under the head of whipping a Performance into Shape.

When the two Geniuses sat out in front they recognized nothing except the Scenery and Costumes.

Their idyllic Creation had been mangled into a roughhouse Riot, in which Disorderly Conduct alternated with the shameless Gyrations taught in San Francisco.

The last Act had been omitted altogether without affecting the coherency of the Story.

The Plot died just four minutes after the Ring-Up.

Although the Report showed 27 Encores and the Gate began to jump $80 a Night, both the intellectual Troubadour and the Student of Counter- Harmonies went to the Manager and cried on his Shoulder and said that their Beautiful work had been ruined.

He called attention to the Chunk of Money tied up in Silk Tights and fireproof Borders.

When it came to a show-down between Dough and Art he didn't propose to tear up his Meal Ticket.

If they would beat it and stay hid and leave the Artists fatten up their Scenes, probably the Bloomer could be converted into a Knock-Out.

While they were in the Sanitarium, the former Minstrel King and young Abie Fixit from the Music Foundry cut out the last vestiges of the Original Stuff and put in two Turns that had landed strong over the whole Orpheum Circuit.

The romantic Operetta now became known as Another One of Those Things.

It was eagerly discussed by Club Women and College Students.

Good seats down in the Observation Rows were not to be had except at the Hotel News Stand.

The Litry Guy and the Music-Maker came out of the Rest Cure to learn that they had registered a Hit and could get their names in "Who's Who."

With the Royalty Checks coming in from the eastern Centers of Culture they were enabled to buy four-cylinder Cars with which to go riding in lonesome Country Lanes, far from the sight of a Bill-Board.

When the Number Two Company came along presenting the Metropolitan Success in the One-Nighters, the reincarnated

Gilbert and Sullivan packed up their Families and escaped to French Lick.

It was a Sell-Out, because all the Members of the Research Club wanted to see that new Dido called the Chicken Flop.

There was no knocking at the Dutch Lunches that night.

Every one said the Show was a Bint, but they thought it was up to the Author to resign from the Baptist Church.

MORAL: In elevating the Drama be sure to get it High enough, even if you have to make it a trifle Gamey.

THE NEW FABLE OF THE WANDERING BOY
AND THE WAYWARD PARENT

Once there was a story-book Stripling who uncoupled himself from a Yahoo Settlement and moseyed up to the Congested Crossings and the Electric Signs. In due time he returned, wearing Gloves and with his Teeth full of Gold.

Ever since that historic Example it has been the daily desire of the Yokel, staked down in a County Seat, to walk in on Judge Gary and form a Partnership.

It befell that after a High School Alumnus had gone to a Varsity and scaled the fearsome heights of Integral and Differential Calculus, he came home to get some more of Father's Shirts and Handkerchiefs and take a new Slant at Life's doubtful Vista, while getting his Board for nothing.

The Town of his Nativity did not occupy many Pages in the statistical Census Reports. In fact, all the travelling Troupers who had worked for K. and E. referred to it as a Lime, which is the same as a Lemon, only smaller.

The ambitious Bachelor of Arts had a lot of Geological Data and College Fraternity Lore stowed away under his Mortar-Board. His hopes were set on something more noble than a Chair and a Table and a Blotter in a dusty Office up the Stairway leading to Odd Fellows' Hall.

So he resolved to hit the long Trail leading to a Modern

Babylon where the Evening papers were on the Streets before Noon.

He figured that a Gazimbat with a John C. Calhoun Forehead and a lot of inside Dope on Hindoo Anthology could break into almost any Reservoir of Culture and bring home the Bacon.

Parents were dead willing to have him migrate and take his Tailor Bills with him, but they shivered with Dread when it came time to ship him to Gomorrah.

They knew all about the unbridled Deviltry of the City, having seen the large colored Illustrations in the Sunday Papers.

They had it on good Authority that the whole sub-stratum of Urban Existence was honeycombed with Rathskellers, while a Prominent Actress waited on almost every Corner, soliciting Travel on the Taxicab Route to the everlasting Coke Ovens.

While Elmer's fragile Steamer Trunk was being hoisted into the Dray, all the Relations who had assisted in bringing him up by Hand clustered around the melodeon and sang, "Oh, where is my Boy to-night?"

After the Day Coach had pulled away from the Depot, he opened the Shoe-Box to extract a Crull and found a Book written by T. DeWitt Talmage, in which many Passages were marked.

He arrived at Union Station with his Fingers crossed. He told himself that he would break into a Dog Trot every time Vice beckoned to him. After he had hung up his Diploma and Razor Strop in the third-story Recess of a very naughty Beanery, he hunted up some of the dear old Pals with whom he had bunked in the Dorm.

They told him they would put him next to a lot of nice clean People. He began to tremble, fearing that some one was about to offer him Champagne, but the Orgy to which they conducted him was merely a meeting of the Civic Purifiers in a basement underneath a Church. He had not expected to find any Churches in the great wicked City. He thought each side of the Street would be built up solidly with Syndicate Theatres, Bacchanalian Bazaars, and Manicure Pitfalls.

Instead of finding Vice triumphant, he learned that it was being chased up an Alley by the entire Police Force and the Federation of Women's Clubs.

He had the gift of Gab and a natural thirst for Tea, and the first thing he knew he had been drawn into so many Campaigns for Social Betterment that he had no time to hunt up conventional Temptations, such as the Welsh Rabbit or the Musical Comedy.

He found himself sitting next to a new type of Lassie. She had no Heels on her Shoes, pronounced each Syllable distinctly, and believed that her Mission in Life was to carry Maeterlinck to the Masses.

In nearly every Instance she had a Father who acted as frozen Figurehead for some Trust Company.

Consequently, Elmer began to perk up and serve on Committees which met in Exclusive Homes and were entirely surrounded by Mahogany.

Whenever an Intellectual Queen pushed the Button, Elmer was right there with a Pitcher of Ice Water.

His Researches had proved to him that one of the Keenest Enjoyments of City Life is to remain away from the glaring Lobster Palace, especially when one can get one's Mallard Duck free of charge in a Flat renting for $6000 a Year.

Elmer became identified with the Cleaning Brigade of the Reform Element simply by riding on the Current of Events.

Adapting himself unconsciously to his antisepticized Environment, he acquired the Art of putting over the saccharine Extemporaneous Address, and he could smile, with his Teeth exposed, for an Hour at a time. In fact, he was a great Success.

At first he took in the Symphony Orchestra because he was dragged thither. After about two years the Virus had permeated his System, and he was a regular Brahmsite. If he didn't get a full dose of Peer Gynt every few days, he was as nervous as a Cat.

The tall and straight-grained Heiress who finally landed him was only too glad to slip him the Bank-Book and tell him to go and sit in with the other Directors.

And now, having become a shiny Pillar in the Presbyterian Temple and one of the most respected Umbrella-Carriers on the Avenue, he felt a longing to beat it back to the home Burg and exhibit his Virtues to the members of the I-Knew-Him-When Club.

He wanted to patronize the Friends of his Youth and note the Expressions of Discomfiture on the so-called Faces of Aunt Lib and Uncle Jethro, both of whom had told around that he was a Gnat (Net) and never would amount to a Hill of Beans.

Elmer expected to find the same spotted Dog asleep in front of the Commercial Hotel and the same Stick Candy exhibited in the Show Windows.

But, while he had been witnessing the downfall of Evil in the busy Metropolis, the Home Town had been putting on a little Side-Show of its own.

Along at the gateway of the 20th Century, every undersized Hamlet shown in the Atlas became seized with a Desire to throw on City Lugs.

The same Father who had marked the Talmage Book for

Elmer became Chairman of the House Committee in a Club which undertook to serve anything usually found on either side of a Cash Register.

Being in the heart of the Residence District, this select Organization could not obtain a regular License.

However, having the moral support of the Best People, it maintained a Blind Pig.

The combination of Blind Pig, two playful Kitties up-stairs, and a lot of gay Dogs spread out on the upholstered Chairs, certainly proved to be some Menagerie.

It was a matter of Pride with the Members that the Colored Boy could shake up anything known to the Regular Trade at the Knickerbocker or the Plaza.

One of their main Delights, also, was to welcome the Stranger, who thought he was sojourning among the Rubes, and lead him into the Roodle Department, the purpose being to get him out on a Limb and then saw off the Limb.

Poker was written in a Small Town. The Hay-Mow Graduate with a limited Income, who counts up every Night and sets aside so much for Wheat Cakes, can hold them closer to his Bosom and play them tighter than any Shark that ever floated down the Mississippi.

The newcomer who tried to be Liberal usually went home in his Stocking Feet.

Day by Day the Progressive Element in the Community widened its Horizon, and the Country Club became a Necessity.

The 9-hole Course was laid out by a Scotch Professional, and every Locker contained something besides Clubs.

When the Church Bells were ding-donging at 10 A. M. on Sunday, the former teacher of the Bible Class and the back-sliding Basso of the Choir would be zig-zagging around the Links, the Stake being a Ball a Hole.

Elmer's Father became a Demon with the Irons and had his Name engraved on a Consolation Cup.

Simultaneous with the Golf Epidemic, a good many Families that could not afford Kitchen Cabinets began to glide around in red Touring-Cars. Any one smelling the Blue Smoke along Main Street and then looking both ways before dashing across to the Drug Store was compelled to admit that the Jays had awakened from their Long Sleep.

Refined Vawdyville was on tap daily, and the Children of those who were only moderately well-to-do knew all the latest improper Songs.

While the men were changing from Jumpers to Tuxedos, the Sisters had not remained stationary.

The Lap Supper was formally abolished soon after Puff Sleeves went out. Girls who had been brought up on Parchesi and Muggins would sit around the Bridge Table all afternoon, trying to cop out some Lace for the new Party Dress.

An imported Professor taught the Buds how to Tango and Trot.

Within a week after a new one had horrified Newport, the Younger Set would have it down pat and be mopping up the floor with one another. Of course they were denounced by the local Ministers, but the Guilty Parties never heard the Denunciations, as they were out Motoring at the time.

Whenever there was a Big Session, all Bridles were removed and the Speed Limit abolished.

Riding home in the Livery Hacks about 4 A. M., the Merry-Makers would be all in, but much gratified to know that Vienna and Paree had nothing on them as regards Rough House.

All the Elite would get together and open a Keg of Spikes at the slightest Provocation.

It was remarkable how much Dull Care they could banish in one Evening, especially if they got an Early Start.

The Town Pump did a punk Business, but the Side-Boards blossomed with Fusel Oil and Fizzerine.

Intense Excitement prevailed when word came that Elmer was En Route. Little Knots of People could be seen standing on the Corners, framing a Schedule of Entertainment which involved nearly everything except Sleep.

They said to themselves: "It is up to us to show this proud Pill from the City that we can be a bit Goey when the Going is right. If he thinks he can pull any new Wrinkles on the Provincials, he is entitled to another Think. We must get into our Evening Glads early this Afternoon and clear the Decks for a Hard Night."

While they were making these grim Preparations, Elmer was doubled up in Section 8, reading a sterilized Magazine from Boston. Subconsciously he counted the peaceful Days that would ensue.

He figured on going back to the dear old Room under the Eaves, with a patch-work Quilt on the Four-Poster and a Steel Engraving of U. S. Grant on the Wall.

Having devoted many Days to the Annual Report of the Purity Brigade, he was due to turn in at 9 o'clock each evening, while recuperating in the Country.

The sanctified Product of the new and regenerative Influences at work in every City was plunked down in the Hot-bed of Gaiety at about 4 P. M..

The Comrades of his Boyhood were massed on the Platform. As he alighted, they sang, "Hail! Hail! the gang's All Here!" and so on and so on.

They had acquired a Running Start. It was their belief that Elmer would be gratified to know that all the Elect had become slightly spiffed in his Honor.

They sent his Stuff up to the House, crowded Two-Weeks' Cards into his Pockets, and bore him away in a Town Car to the Club, where Relays were waiting to extend Hospitality to the returned Exile until he was Plastered.

They seemed to think he had devoted the years of his Absence to building up a Thirst.

Their Dismay was genuine when he timidly informed the Irrigation Committee that he desired Vichy.

They told him he was a Celluloid Sport and that his refusal to Libate was little short of an Affront.

Escaping from the Comanches, he hurried to the Old Homestead to sit by the Grate Fire and tease the Cat.

He found Pa and Ma dolled up like a couple of aristocratic Equines, much Awning over the Front Stoop, and strange Waiters hot-footing through the Hallways.

In order to make it seem as much like the City as possible, they had ribbed up a swell combination Gorge and Deluge, to be followed by an Indoor Circus, a Carnival of Terpsichorean Eccentricities, and a correct Reproduction of Monte Carlo at the height of the Season.

Therefore, when their Only Child suggested that he would fain hie to the Husks at a Reasonable Hour, they told him that Slumber was made for Slaves and to take his Feet out of his Lap and move around.

Having led a sheltered Life among the devotees of Jane Addams and Jacob Riis, he was dazed and horrified to find himself suddenly subjected to the demoralizing Influences of the Small Town.

They scoffed at him when he said that his regular twilight Repast was a saucer of granose Flakes, a mere sliver of White Meat, and some diluted Milk.

His home was near the White Light District, and they just knew that he was accustomed to bathe in the Bubbles.

He sat back benumbed for many hours watching the wicked Rustics perform.

He had read about such things in the reports of the Commission, but this was the first time that he had ever really been Slumming.

When he weakened on the Bumper Proposition and disavowed any familiarity with the Texas Tommy spasm or the fine points of Auction, the sophisticated ones exchanged significant Glances.

They tumbled to the Fact that Elmer was not such a much, even if he did reside at Headquarters. It was evident that he had not been travelling with the Real Razmataz Rompers.

He was panned to a Whisper next day. The Verdict was in. Elmer was branded a Dead One.

He is now in the crowded City, trying to arrange to have his rowdy Parents come in and take the Cure.

George Ade

MORAL: Those having the most Time to devote to a Line of Endeavor usually become the most Proficient.

THE NEW FABLE OF WHAT TRANSPIRES
AFTER THE WIND-UP

Once upon a time Ferdinand breathed right into Adele's translucent Listener those three Words which hold all Records as monosyllabic Trouble-Makers.

They have a harmless look on the Printed Page, but when pulled at the Psychological turn of the Road, they become the Funeral Knell of Bachelor Freedom and a Prelude to cutting the String on whatever has been put by.

The Serpent, operating in the guise of a Lover in a Serge Suit, had lured, cajoled, wheedled, and finessed until the poor trembling Child, only twenty-four years of Age, was alone with him in what the Landscaper had worked off on her Papa as a Formal Garden.

They stood clinched there in the dull Sunset Glow, with a Pergola for a Background. It was all very Belasco and in strict compliance with the League Rules laid down by W. Somerset Maugham.

According to the $2 Drama and every bright red Volume selling for $1.18 at a Department Store, this was

THE END

The Curtain began to descend very slowly, with Ferdinand and Adele holding the Picture.

It seems, however, that they had not come to the real, sure-enough Finis. The Terminus was some distance down the Line.

The Curtain refused to fall.

"What is the idea?" asked Adele, somewhat perturbed. "We have hit the logical Climax of our Romance. As I understand it, we are now supposed to ascend in a Cloud and float through Ethereal Bliss for an indefinite Period."

"Right-o!" said the Fiance. "According to all the approved Dope, we are booked to live happily ever after."

Just then Her Best Friend came rapidly down the Gravel Walk with Anxiety stenciled on her Features.

The accepted Swain seemed to hear a low rumbling Wagnerian Effect from out the Clear Sky. In Music-Drama it is known as the Hammer Theme. It is included in the Curriculum at every Fem Sem.

Ferdinand had a Hunch that somebody was getting ready to drop Cyanide of Potassium into his Cup of Joy.

"Oh, Adele!" said the Friend, just like that. "Oh, Adele, may I speak to you for a Mo-munt?"

Ferdinand made his Exit, much peeved, and the Friend expressed a Hope that she had arrived in time to throw the Switch and avert the Wrecking of a Life.

Far be it from her to Snitch, but it was her Duty to put Adele wise to what every one was whispering Under Cover.

She had no absolute Proof that he had carried on with a Front Row Floss in New Haven, but it was Common Talk that one of his Uncles had been a Regular at a Retreat where the Doctor shoots a Precious Metal into the Arm.

It would be terrible to marry someone and then find out that he Drank, the same as all the other Married Men.

Leaving Adele in a Deep Swoon, the true Friend hurried to the nearest Public 'Phone to spread the dismal Tidings.

In the meantime the elated Lover had loped all the way to the University club to spring it on the Navajos and receive their Felicitations.

His Rapture had rendered him fairly incoherent, and he was gurgling like an after-dinner Percolator; but he finally made it evident that he had been Hooked.

A deep Silence ensued, most of those present looking out the Window at the passing Traffic.

Finally a Shell-Back, who had been leading a Life of Single Torment ever since Sumter was fired upon, asked in a sepulchral Tone and without looking up from his Hand, "Has the Date been set?"

Ferdinand tried to tell them that he was going to the Altar and not to the Electric Chair, but he couldn't get a single Slap on the Back.

The only one evincing Interest was a He-Hen named Herbert, who took him into the Cloak-Room to plant a few Canadian Thistles in the Garden of Love.

Herb said he had always liked the Girl, even if she had given a couple of his Best Pals the Whillykathrow.

His Advice was to up and marry her before she had time to pull one of her temperamental Stunts and hand out the Rinkaboo.

Possibly if she could be weaned away from her eccentric Relations and governed with a Firm Hand she would turn out O. K..

Still, it was a tall Gamble. Under the Circumstances, he didn't see that there was anything for Ferdinand to do except mop up a few Drinks and hope for the Best.

When Ferdy looked at himself in the Mirror at Midnight, he didn't know whether he was Engaged or merely operating under a Suspended Sentence.

Next morning he had to bare his Soul to the Head of the Firm. This revered Fluff should have been known as Mr. Yes-But.

He was strong for the Married State, but it was highly advisable to have the Girl analyzed by a Chemist and passed upon by a Board of Experts before a Bid was submitted.

The Sunflower Paths of Dalliance were leading mostly to Reno, Nevada, and the Article commonly known as Love was merely a disinclination to continue eating Breakfast alone.

He said a Good Woman was a Jewel, but if one of them got a fair Run and Jump at a Check-Book she could put the National City Bank on the Hummer. Probably it was all right to go ahead, and take the High Hurdle, but the Percentage was against the Candidate, and the Cost of Living was never so altitudinous.

Ferdinand retired from the Royal Presence feeling that he had been duly authorized to walk a Tight Rope over Niagara Falls.

As soon as the Bride-Elect had taken enough Headache Powders to prepare her for the Ordeal, she sent for the Suspect to come up to the House and outline his Defense.

They put in a humid Evening. When the falling Tears had made the Drawing-Room too soppy for further use, they moved into the Hallway and he continued to think up Alibis.

At 11 P. M. he had explained Everything, repudiated many lifelong Friendships, deodorized his College Career, flouted the Demon Rum, and resigned from all Clubs.

The Birds were singing up and down the Main Stairway and Grandfather's Clock played nothing but Mendelssohn.

She lay damply pillowed on his Bosom. He was intensely relieved and yet vaguely conscious of the Fact that she had beat him to it. There had been a General Settlement, and he had figured merely as Supreme Goat.

In his anxiety to get the Kinks out of his own Record he had failed to hold her up for anything except a Pardon.

Before terminating the Peace Conference, it was suggested that inasmuch as every one else in the World had been notified, probably it would be just as well to let her Male Parent in on the Secret. Not that Father is regarded as a Principal in the up-to-date Household. Still, he is useful as a Super.

The old Gentleman was so soft that he nearly tipped his Hand. He gave Ferdinand a regular Cigar and then stalled for about 30 Seconds before indicating a Willingness to sign any form of Contract.

He pulled the Old One to the effect that the House would not seem the same after Addie had gone away, meaning that Breakfast would be served in the Morning and the Night Shift abolished.

When Ferdinand got back to his Room and counted up, he had to admit that Father was the only Outsider who seemed to be plugging for the Alliance.

But all petty Suspicions and unworthy Doubts flickered and disappeared when Nightfall came and Queenie was once more cuddled within the strong right Fin, naming over some of the Men that he mustn't speak to any more.

George Ade

The course of True Love ran smooth for a couple of Days, and then came a letter from his People, expressing the hope that he had picked out a devout Unitarian. Otherwise the Progeny would start off under a terrible Handicap.

He knew that Adele favored the Suffrage Thing and that she had read a Book on how to recover from a Dance by lying down and giving a Recitation, but he never had suspected her of any real Religious Scruples.

Before he could tell her how the Little Ones had been predestined, she notified him that her kinsmen had been peering into the Future and that all the problematical Offspring had been put on the Waiting List at the First Baptist Church.

Here was a grand Opening for Ferdinand. He resolved to make a Stand and issue a ringing Ultimatum. He might as well tip it off to her and the whole Tribe that he was to be Caesar in his own Shack.

So he went up to her House ready to die in the last ditch rather than yield to the advocates of Immersion. After viewing the Problem in all its Aspects, he and Honey compromised by deciding that the Bairns were to be orthodox Baptists.

Having sponged every Blot from the Escutcheon and laid out the Labels for all Generations yet unborn, the incipient Benedick thought there would be nothing more to it except Holding Hands and watching the Calendar.

Just then a Dress-Maker swooped down and stole away the Light of his Life.

Every time he went up to scratch on the Door and beg for a Kiss, a Strange Lady with Pins in her Mouth would come out and shoo him away, explaining that the Pearl of Womanhood was laid out in the Operating Room, being measured for something additional.

Occasionally he saw her, at one of the many Dinners decreed by Custom. They had to sit Miles apart, with Mountains of unseemly Victuals stacked between them, while some moss-grown Offshoot of the Family Tree rose and conquered his Asthma long enough to propose a Toast to the Bride.

What they really craved was a Dim Corner and a box of Candied Cherries.

The only Speeches they wished to hear could have been constructed out of the 40 words of standard Baby Talk, comprising what is known as the Mush Vocabulary.

Yet they had to muster the same old property Smile every time that Charley Bromide or old Mr. Platitude lifted a shell of sparkling Vinegar and fervently exclaimed, "Thuh Bride!"

Even after the Menu had been wrecked and the satiated Revelers had laboriously pried themselves away from the decorated Board, there was no escape.

The Women Folks led Adele away to some remote Apartment to sound a Few Warnings, while the Men sat around in the Blue Smoke and joshed Ferdinand to a fare-ye-well.

Each morning he found in his Mail a few Sealed Orders from Headquarters and about as many Stage Directions as would be required for putting on the Annual Show at the Hippodrome.

When he was not begging some one to come and Ush for him, he was either checking over the Glove List with a terrified Best Man or getting measured for a full layout of dark Livery that made him look like a refined Floor-Walker.

It seemed that Adele had a Step-Mother who had been crouched for Years waiting for a chance to bust into the Papers. Nothing would do her but a regular Madison Square Phantasmagoria, with two Rings and an elevated Platform.

She wanted Ribbons down the Aisle and little Girls sprinkling Posies, a Concert Orchestra buried under the Palms, and a few extra Ministers of the Gospel just to dress the Pulpit.

Every superfluous Accessory devised by the Nerve Specialist and approved by the Court of Bankruptcy was woven into the Nuptial Circus when Ferdinand and Adele were made one and Unhookable.

The Rehearsals somewhat resembled the Moving Pictures of the Durbar at Delhi.

As a final Preparation for the Stupendous Pageant, the Groom sat up all night in the Dipsomania Club, watching the Head-Liners of the Blue Book demolish Glassware.

According to the dictates of Fashion, one who is about to assume the solemn Responsibilities of Matrimony should abstain from Slumber for a week, devoting the time thus saved to a full consideration of Food and Drink.

The Ambulance bore his Remains to the Church. A few faithful Hang-Overs lifted him through the Portals, with his Toes dragging somewhat in the Rear.

They propped him against a Pilaster and told him his Name and begged him not to weaken, no matter what the Preacher might put up to him. Soon after he saw a Haggard Creature all fluffed about with White advancing unsteadily toward him. With the Make-Up, she did not look a Day over 47.

He did not hear any of the Service, but those who were more fortunate told him afterward that it was a very Pretty Wedding, and that they Presents they got were Simply Great.

MORAL: Too many Trained Nurses discommode Cupid.

THE DREAM THAT CAME OUT
WITH MUCH TO BOOT

Once there was a provincial Tradesman who gave his Yokemate a Christmas Present. It was a kind of Dingus formerly exhibited on the What-Not in almost every polite Home.

By peering through at the twin Photographs and working it like a Slide Trombone, one could get ravishing glimpses of Trafalgar Square, Lake Como, and the Birthplace of Bobby Burns.

Nearly every evening the Tradesman would back up to the Student Lamp and put in a delirious half-hour with the Views.

While gazing up the Rue de Rivoli or across the rice paddies at the snowy cap of Fuji, his Blood would become het by the old boyhood Desire to sail across the Blue to Foreign Parts.

Those who saw him mowing the Lawn little suspected that he was being inwardly eaten by the Wanderlust.

The Tradesman, Edwin by name, and his Managing Director, Selena, formed the magic-lantern Habit away back in the days of Stoddard. They never missed a chance to take in Burton Holmes. Sitting in the darkness, they would hold hands and simply eat those Colored Slides.

Selena belonged to a Club that was trying to get a side-hold on

George Ade

the Art and Architecture of the Old World. She had a smouldering Ambition to ride a Camel in the Orient and then come home and put it all over a certain proud Hen who had spent six weeks in Europe.

One visit to Niagara Falls and a glorious week of Saengerfest at Cincinnati had simply whetted her desire to take Edwin by the hand and beat it all the way around the Globe, via Singapore. To prepare herself for the Grand Tour, she took 12 lessons in French and read up on the Taj Mahal.

She had to wait patiently until Edwin was threatened with a Nervous Break-Down. At last the Happy Day arrived when the Specialist told him he must make his choice between a long Sea Voyage and a slow ride to the Family Lot.

Selena used Hydraulic Pressure in packing her Wardrobe Trunks. She took all her circus Duds and a slew of Hats so that she could make the proper Front, while being entertained Abroad.

Edwin had secured a Passport which identified him as a male white Person, entitled to all the Courtesies and Privileges usually extended to an American Citizen holding a Passport.

They were on the verge of the Jumps when they boarded the Train, but they hoped to Relax and get a lot of Sleep on the Ocean Greyhound.

A few days later they were curled up in a Cabin de Luxe about the size of a Telephone Booth, waiting for the Ocean Greyhound to recover from an attack of Hydrophobia.

When they tottered down the Gang-Plank, after six days on the playful North Atlantic, their only Comfort was derived from the knowledge that, as soon as they had rested up, they could write home and quote the Second Officer as saying it was the roughest Passage he had ever Known.

After spending a few days in London trying to get warm, they moved on to Paris, which they remembered long afterward on account of Napoleon's Tomb and the price of Strawberries.

Selena pulled her tall-grass French on a Hackman, but there was nothing doing. He had taken it from a different Teacher.

So they employed a Guide who knew all the Shops. If Selena happened to admire a Trinket or some outre Confection with Lace slathered on it, a perfumed Apache in a Frock Coat would take Edwin into a side room, give him the sleeve across the Wind-Pipe, and bite a piece out of his Letter of Credit.

Edwin did a little quick work with the Pencil and said they could either hurry on or else hie back to the Home Town and begin Life all over again.

Three weeks after saying good-bye to Griddle Cakes they were in Naples, which they had seen pictured on so many Calendars.

Looking back across the Centuries they recalled the Clerks standing in the Doorways and the friends of the Progressive Euchre Club. It was sweet to remember that the world was not made up entirely of cadging Head Waiters.

Once in a while they would venture from the Hotel to run footraces with the yelping Lazzaroni or try to look at Vesuve without paying seven or eight members of the Camorra for the Privilege.

After being chased back into the Hotel, they would sit down and address Post-Cards by the Hour, telling how much they were enjoying the stay in Napoli, home of Song and Laughter.

Their only chance of catching even on the Imperial Suite at $9 a Day was to make the Folks back at the Whistling Post think they were playing Guitars and dancing the Tarantella, whatever that is.

Next we see them in Egypt, still addressing Post-Cards, and offering anything within Reason for a good Cup of Coffee.

Somehow, sitting in the dusky Tombs didn't seem to help their Nostalgia. Not that they would own up to being Home-Sick. No, indeed! They kept writing back that they enjoyed every Minute spent among the Cemeteries and Ruins, or sailing up the Nile, and Edwin was holding up wonderfully, for an Invalid.

Only, when either of them spoke of the Children, or Corned-Beef Hash, or the Canary, a long Silence would ensue, and then the Nervous Wreck would cheer her by computing that they would be in God's Country within four months, if they escaped Shipwreck, Sunstroke, and Bubonic Plague.

While parboiling themselves down the Red Sea it began to soak in on them that, east of Suez, the Yank has about as much standing as the Ten Commandments.

They could have endured sleeping in a Trough and bathing with a damp Towel and eating Food kept over from the year before, if their Fellow Voyagers had made a slight fuss over them or evinced some interest in the wonders of North America.

The Congressman at home had assured them, on numerous occasions, that Columbia was the Jim of the Ocean and the most upholstered portion of the entire Foot-Stool.

Consequently, it was somewhat disconcerting to meet British subjects who never had heard of Quincy, Illinois, and who moved their Deck Chairs every time they were given a chance to hear about it.

Back in the Middle West, Edwin and Selena had been Mountains arising from the Plain. At all points beyond Greenwich, they were simply two unconsidered fragments of Foreign Substance.

The Passport did not seem to get them anything. While being walked upon by the haughty Tea-Drinkers they could not claim the protection of the American Flag, because they didn't see the Starry Banner after leaving New York, except in front of a Fake Auction Sale, arranged especially for Tourists.

By the time they found themselves in that vast bake-oven known as India they were benumbed and submissive and had settled into a Routine. They would arrive in a New Town, fly to the Hotel, unpack, go out and buy their colored Post-Cards, come back to the Dump (usually called the Grand Hotel Victoria), address Cards to all the Names on the list, then pack up, pay the Overcharges, and ride to the Railway Station, accompanied by a small regiment of Bashi-Bazouks who were looking for Theirs.

The sight of a Temple threw Edwin into a Relapse, but he would have given $8,000 for one look at the galvanized Cornice of the Court House. Selena was still buying Souvenirs, but doing it mechanically, as if in a Trance.

They had been stung with so many Oriental Phoneys and stuck up so often that they had gone Yellow and lost their Nerve.

When they saw an outstretched Palm, they came across without a Whimper.

Cousin Ella, back among the Corn Fields, pictured them as riding a caparisoned Elephant up to the marble Palace of the Gackwar of Baroda, where Edwin would flash his Passport and then the distinguished Guests would be salaamed to the Peacock Throne.

Nothing like it. They were led up to highly odorous Bazaars conducted by lineal Descendants of the 40 Thieves.

Often, while riding in the dusty Cattle Cars and looking out at the parched Plains, they would think of the shaded Front

Porch, only 5 minutes from Barclay's Drug Store, where they sold the Ice Cream Soda. Moaning feebly, they would return to the italicized Guide Book.

The Chow consisted largely of Curry and Rice, the medicinal flavor of which was further accentuated by Butter brought in Tins all the way from Sweden.

Although the Heat was intense, they found occasional Relief in sitting next the Britons and getting a few Zephyrs direct from the Ice-Box.

Each day they would purchase a News-paper about the size of a Bed-Spread and search eagerly for American News. Once in a while they would learn that Congress had met or another Colored Person had been burned at the Stake. It cheered them immensely to know that the Land of the Free was still squirming.

At Rangoon they met a weary Countryman headed in the opposite direction. He was a hard-faced Customer who was fighting the Climate with Gin and Bitters, but they fell upon him and wanted to Kiss him when they learned that he had once met Selena's Uncle at Colorado Springs.

They told him how to save time in getting across India, and he gave them a list of Places in China and Japan that might be dodged to advantage.

Year after year in the months of March and April they continued on their tedious Way through the burning Tropics.

Sometimes they came to a discouraged belief that the World was one bluey expanse, disturbed by Flying Fish.

Then they would spend weary Ages along the avenues of white Lime-Kilns, looking at Countless millions of hungry Brunettes in fluttering Nighties.

Their principal Occupation, when not setting down Expressions of Delight on the Post-Cards, was to study Time-Tables and cable ahead for Reservations.

The Invalid's one desire was to get home and take a regular Bath before being laid out.

Hong Kong pleased them exceedingly because they learned, by consulting Mr. Mercator's Projection, that they were on the Home Stretch and, with Luck in their favor, might live to see another Piece of Huckleberry Pie.

Japan they liked best of all. At Yokohama they received a bundle of Dailies only six weeks old, giving full Particulars of a Wedding and telling who was about to run for Mayor.

As soon as they were on the Pacific and headed for a refined Vaudeville Show, they began to recover the brave Spirit of Travel and blow about what they had seen.

The Towns and Temples and Tombs and Treasures of Art were all jumbled together, but, by daily references to Baedeker and Murray, they were enabled to find out where they had been and what they had seen with their own eyes and how it impressed them at the time.

Before touching at Honolulu they were real enthusiastic about India. They advised the awe-stricken Listener who had not been all the Way around to be sure and take in Penang and Johore and, if necessary, they would give him Letters of Introduction.

They said it had been a Wonderful Experience. Yes, indeed. And broadening. Very. Then Edwin would wander to the front end of the Ship and want to climb out on the Bowsprit so as to be in Frisco ahead of anybody else.

He convalesced rapidly as they approached the Golden Gate, for he knew that in a few days he would unpack for good and gallop down to the office and not have to worry about Travelling.

The only Dark Cloud on the Shore hung above the Custom House. They looked at all the Junk wished upon them by the simple Children of the Far East and didn't know whether to declare it for what it cost or for what it was really worth.

Being conscientious Members of the Church, they modified their Perjury and smuggled only the usual amount of Carvings and hand-embroidered Stuff.

Two hours after landing, Edwin saw a Porter-House Steak and burst into tears.

They sped eastward by the first Train, still busy with the little Red Books, for they knew they would have to answer a lot of Questions. "Shall we own up and tell them the Awful Truth?" asked Selena.

"Not on your Esoteric Buddhism," replied Edwin. "We never will be rewarded for our Sufferings unless we convince the Neighbors that we had a run for our Money. It was a troubled Nightmare, in Spots, but when I lecture in the Church Parlor I am going to burn Joss Sticks and pull every variety of Bunk made famous by Sir Edwin Arnold and Lafcadio Hearn."

On the following Tuesday, Selena appeared at the Club with her Mandarin Coat and the long Hindoo Ear-Rings. She had them frozen in their Chairs.

MORAL: Be it ever so Hard to Take, there is no Place like away from Home.

THE NEW FABLE OF THE TOILSOME ASCENT
AND THE SHINING TABLE-LAND

Once upon a time, out in the Rubber Boot Reservation, the Stork came staggering up to a Frame Dwelling with a hefty Infant. The arrival was under the Zodiacal Sign of Taurus, the Bull. Every Omen was propitious. When the Gallery was admitted, on the third day, the gaping Spectators observed that the Youngun had an open Countenance, somewhat like a Channel Cat, a full head of Hair bushing at the nape of the neck, and a hypnotic Eye; so they knew he was destined for the Service of the Public.

Even while he was in the custody of the Old Women of the Township, he began reaching for everything he saw and testing his Voice. He claimed his Rations frequently and with insistence.

While he was demonstrating an elastic Capacity, the head Prophetess called attention to his aggressive Style and predicted a political Career.

It was a cinch Horoscope, for the Begetters were a successful Auctioneer and a Poetess of local repute.

The Child was christened Sylvester, in anticipation of his Future Greatness.

Several years later, when he rebelled against going to the Barber Shop and began to speak Pieces on the slightest provocation, the Parents rejoiced over these budding symptoms of Statesmanship and bought him a Drum.

At school he was a Dummy in Mathematics and a Lummox when it came to Spelling Down, but every Friday afternoon he was out in the lead, wearing Bells.

Before he acquired a Vocabulary or accumulated Data, he got by on his Nerve. In later years he never forgot that Facts are non-essential if the Vocal Cords are in tune.

When the Pupils tacked the old standby, "Resolved, that Education is better than Riches," he could tremolo on the Affirmative one week and then reverberate for the Negative one week later, never doubting his own Sincerity at any stage of the Game.

The grinding classmates who had secured the mark of A in Geometry and Rhetoric were not in the running on Commencement Day.

Our Hero got his Diploma on a Fluke, but when he appeared on the Rostrum between an Oleander and the Members of the Board, with Goose-Goose on the Aureole, the new Store Suit garnished with a leaf of Geranium and a yellow Rose-Bud, and the Gates Ajar Collar lashed fast with his future Trade-Mark: viz., a White Bow Tie—he had all the Book Worms crushed under his Heel.

He pulled out the stop marked "Vox Humana" and begged his Hearers to lift the sword of Justice and with it smite the Deluge of Organized Wealth which was crouched and ready to spring upon the Common People. In pleading the cause of Labor, he spoke as an expert, for once he had strung a Clothes-Line for his Mother.

He got the biggest Hand of any one at the Exercises. After denouncing the predaceous Interests he relapsed into an attitude of Meditation, with the Chin on the starched Front, very much like a Steel Engraving of Daniel Webster.

The enthralled Townsmen, seeing him thus, with the Right Hand buried in the Sack Suit and the raven Mop projecting in the rear, allowed that there was nothing to it. He was a Genius and billed through for the Legislature.

Some Boys have to go to College to get a Shellac Finish, but Sylvester already had the Dark Clothes and the Corrugated Brow and a voice like a Tuba, so, to complete his Equipment, he merely had to sit tilted back in a Law Office for a few months and then borrow Money to get a Hat such as John A. Logan used to wear.

All who saw him move from Group to Group along the Hitch Rack on Saturday afternoon, shaking hands with the Rustics and applying the Ointment, remarked that Ves was a young man of Rare Promise and could not be held back from the Pay-Roll for any considerable length of Time. He was one of the original 787 Boy Orators of the Timothy Hay Section of the Imperial Middle West.

At every hotel Banquet, whether by the Alumni of the Shorthand College or under the auspices of the Piano Movers' Pleasure Club, he was right up at the Head Table with his Hair rumpled, ready to exchange a Monologue for a few warm Oysters and a cut of withered Chicken.

On Memorial Day it was Sylvester who choked up while laying his Benediction on the Cumrads of the G. A. R..

On Labor Day he unbuttoned his Vest all the way down, held a trembling Fist clear above the leonine Mat, and demanded a living Wage for every Toiler.

Consequently he acquired repute as a Staunch Friend of the Agriculturist, the Steam Fitter, the Old Soldier, the Department Store Employee, and others accustomed to voting in Shoals. In order to mature himself and be seasoned for onerous

Responsibilities, he waited until he was 22 years of age before attempting to gain a frontage at the Trough.

It was highly important that he should serve the Suvrin People in some Capacity involving Compensation. It was fairly important to him and it was vitally important to a certain Woman of gambling Disposition, who operated a Boarding-House.

Sylvester was the type of Lawyer intensely admired but seldom employed, save by Criminals entirely bereft of Means.

In addition to his Board, the young Barrister actually required a pouch of Fine Cut and a clean White Tie every week, so he was impelled by stern Necessity to endeavor to hook up with a Salary.

Because Sylvester had administered personal Massage to every Voter within five Miles of his office, he thought he could leap into the Arena and claim an immediate Laurel Wreath by the mere charm and vigor of his Personality.

He ignored the Whispering Ikes who met in the dim Back Room, with Cotton plugged in the Key Hole.

The Convention met, and when it came time to nominate a Candidate for State's Attorney, all of Sylvester's tried and true Friends among the Masses were at home working in the Garden and spread out in the Hammock. The Traction Engine pulled the Juggernaut over the Popular Idol.

They lit on him spraddled out. They gave him the Doo-Doo.

When the Battle had ended, he was a mile from the cheerful Bivouac, lying stark in the Moonlight.

He was supposed to be eliminated. The only further recognition accorded him would be at the Autopsy.

Next day he was back in his usual Haunts, with an immaculate Bow Tie and a prop Smile, shaking hands with all who had so recently harpooned him. As a Come-Back he was certainly the resilient Kid.

Those who had marveled at his sole-leather Organ of Speech, now had to admire his sheet metal Sensibilities, nor could they deny that he possessed all the attributes of a sound and durable Candidate.

He had learned his Primer lesson in Politics. As soon as he saw that he could not throw the Combination, he joined it.

He came into the Corral and lay down in the Dust and allowed them to brand him as a Regular.

Sylvester became the White Slave of the Central Committee, knowing that eventually true Patriotism would have to be recognized and recompensed. When he came to bat the second time he had the Permanent Chairman and the Tellers and all the Rough-Necks plugging for him, consequently it was a Pipe.

But it was a case of Reverse English on Election Day, for the venal Opposition rode into power on a Tidal Wave.

After the Tide had receded, Sylvester was found asleep among the Clams and Sea-Weed, apparently so far gone that a Pulmotor would be no help.

Three days later, however, he was on hand, with chaste Neckwear and a jaunty Front, to make a Presentation Speech to the Chief of the Fire Department.

Talk about your Rubber Cores! The harder they run him down the higher he bounced back.

Those who had been marked by Fate to be his Constits began to see that Sylvester was something invincible and not to be denied.

What though his Detractors called him a Four-Flush and a False Alarm, alleging that a true analysis of his Mentality would be just about as profitable as dissecting a Bass Drum?

The more they knocked, the more oleo-margarine became his beaming Countenance, for he knew that Calumny avails naught against a White Tie in the Hot-Bed of cut-and-dried Orthodoxy.

He played the social String from the W. C. T. U. to the Elks and was a blood-brother of the Tin Horn and the acidulated Elder with the scant Skilligans.

In order to keep the High-Binders and the Epworth Leaguers both on his Staff at one and the same time, he had to be some Equilibrist, so he never hoisted a Slug except in his own Office, where he kept it behind the Supreme Court Reports.

When he went out the third time for the same Job, the Voters saw it was no use trying to block him off, so he landed.

In the full crimson of Triumph, with new Patent Leather Shoes and as much as $40 in his Kick at one time, he never forgot for a moment he was a servant of the Pe-hee-pul and might want to run for something else in the near future.

He tempered Justice with Mercy and quashed many an Indictment if the Defendant looked like a grateful Geezer who might be useful in his own Precinct.

No one dared to attack him because of the fact that he had delivered a Lecture to the eager young souls at the Y. M. C. A., in which he had exhibited a Road Map and proved that adherence to the Cardinal Virtues leads unerringly to Success.

At the age of thirty-two he broke into the Legislature and began to wear a White Vest, of the kind affected by the more exclusive Bar Tenders. Also a variety of Shroud known as the Prince Albert. He was fearless in discussing any proposed Measure that did not worry the Farmer Vote in his own District.

As for Wall Street and the Plunder-bund, when he got after them, he was a raving Bosco. A regular Woof-Woofer and bite their heads off.

About the time he came up for re-election, a lot of Character-Assassins tried to shell-road him and hand him the Guff and crowd him into the 9-hole. They said he had been flirting with the Corporations and sitting in on Jack-Pots and smearing himself at the Pie Counter.

Did they secure his Goat by such crude Methods?

Not while the 5-octave Voice and the enveloping Prince Albert and the snow-white Necktie were in working Trim.

He went over the whole District in an Auto (one of the fruits of his Frugality), and everywhere that Sylvester went the American Eagle was sure to go, riding on the Wind-Shield, and a Starry Banner draped over the Hood.

He waved aside all Charges made against him. To give them serious Heed would be an Insult to the high Intelligence of the Hired Hands gathered within Sound of his Voice. He believed in discussing the Paramount Issues.

So he would discuss them in such a way that the Railway Trains passing by were no interruption whatsoever.

In course of time his Hair outgrew the Legislature. He was on whispering terms with a clean majority of all the Partisans in three connecting Counties, so he bought one Gross of the White String Kind and a pair of Gum Sneakers and began to run amuck as a Candidate for Congress.

Even his trusty Henchmen were frightened to know that he had become obsessed of such a vaulting Ambition.

They did not have him sized, that was all. The farther from home he traveled, the more resounding was the Hit he registered.

The Days of Spring were lengthening and the Campaign was not far distant when Sylvester, after looking at the Signs in the Sky and putting his Ear to the Ground, discovered that he was thoroughly impregnated with the new Progressive Doctrines.

The change came overnight, but he was in the Band Wagon ahead of the Driver.

As nearly as he could formulate his private Platform, he was still true to his Party but likewise very keen for any Reform Measure that 55 per cent. of the Voters might favor, either at the present time or previous to any future Election.

After the heated Radicals in every School District had listened to Sylvester and learned that all his Views coincided to a T with their own revised Schedule, they lined up and landslided.

One November morning Our Hero, no longer a penniless Law Student, but owing, at a conservative Estimate, between $6000 and $8000, sat tranquilly in front of the T-Bone Steak, the Eggs, the Batter Cakes, the Cinnamon Rolls, and the Reservoir of Coffee, comprising the Breakfast of one who always remained near to the Rank and File. His Hair was roached in a new way, for the Bulletins at Midnight had told him that he was a Congressman.

Those who had known him in the old Free-Lunch Days, when a Tie lasted him for a Week, now felt honored to receive his stately Salutation as he moved slowly from the Post Office up to the Drug Store, to buy his Bronchial Lozenges.

Many of the Lower Classes, as well as the more Prominent

People belonging to the Silver Cornet Band, were gathered at the Station when he started for Washington to fight in the impending Battle between the Corn-Shuckers and the Allies of Standard Oil.

Men and Women standing right there in the Crowd could remember when he had borrowed his first Dollar.

And now he was going to stand beneath the dome of the Capitol to weave a new Fabric of Government and see that it didn't crock or unravel.

Sylvester and his glossy Trunk arrived at the Mecca, where they were pleasantly received by the Agent of the Transfer Company in full Uniform, and a Senegambian with a Red Cap, who hunted up the Taxi.

After waiting many weary Years, Sylvester once more had a School Desk of his own. It was in the far corner of a crowded Pit surrounded by elevated Seats.

The Hon. Sylvester found himself entirely surrounded by victims of involuntary Dumbness.

By referring to a printed List he ascertained that he was a member of the Committee on Manual Training for the Alaskan Indians.

In his Boarding House he became acquainted with Department Clerks who were well advanced in the technology of Base Ball.

After a few weeks, he was on chatting Terms with a Young Lady in charge of a Cigar and News Counter.

As soon as the Paper was delivered every morning he could find out what had happened in Congress the day before.

If confused by the Cares of State, he sought diversion by

taking a Visitor from Home to see the Washington Monument.

After three months, he met a National Committeeman with a Pull who promised to secure him an introduction to the Speaker so that he could maneuver around and get something into the Record before his time was up.

In the meantime, he is heard to advantage on every Roll Call, and the Traducers back in the District have not been able to lay a finger on anything Crooked.

MORAL: There is always Room and Board at the Top.

THE NEW FABLE OF THE AERIAL PERFORMER,
THE BUZZING BLONDINE, AND
THE DAUGHTER OF MR. JACKSON

Once upon a time a Lad with Cinnamon Hair and wide blue Eyes lived in a half-portion Town.

He had received more than 2000 Tickets for answering "Here" at the M. E. Sunday School.

His kinfolk hoped that some day he would be President of the Town Board.

Shortly after he learned to roll a safe game of Pool, the Governor demised.

Robert, such being the full front name of the sole Heir, found that he could not spread his Pinions in the narrow Streets of the lichen-covered Hamlet.

So he blew. He went to find an Avenue that would accommodate seven Zeppelin Air-Ships moving abreast at one time.

He closed out the Dry Goods Emporium with the Shirt-Waists and the shameless Hosiery in the Windows.

An Apartment Building, with Packages delivered at the rear, soon began to flaunt itself on the site of the old Manse.

With all the currency corralled by the late Store-Keeper

George Ade

padded into his Norfolk Jacket, the gallus Offspring hurried to the Metrop to pick the Primroses.

In a short time he was out at the Track every day, barking at the Goats as they hove into the Stretch.

The pencil-borrowing Touts and the Wine Pushers began to call him Bob, which proved that he was a Man about Town.

When the final Kiflukus was put on the Ponies, he assembled the residue of his Bundle and began to work steady as a Guesser in a Broker's Office.

His job was to show at 10 A. M. with a big Reina Victoria at one extreme corner of his Face and pretend to know what was coming off when the Boy put the funny marks on the Blackboard.

Ever and anon he would buy 1000 Shares of something, as if Negotiating for a Bread-Ticket.

As a rule, the tall-grass Plunger with a wad of new Kale has about the same percentage in his favor as that enjoyed by a Shoat out at the well-known Establishment of Armour & Co.

The Cleaners go forth to meet him, bearing as Gifts a Dream-Book and a new kind of Cocktail with a Kick like a Coast-Defense Gun.

A few weeks later they are casting lots for his Union Suit.

Bob came from Simpville, but he had acquired a couple of Wrinkles associating with the Wing Shots in the Paddock.

He could shift to either Foot and he kept his Maxillary covered.

Sometimes he picked up the wrong Walnut. It would begin to look like a quick change from Caviar to Crackers.

More than once his Heels were beating a tattoo on the grassy brink of a Precipice.

Then he would smell around until he discovered Something Doing. A couple of lucky shots and he would be on Velvet again and whanging away like a Demon.

At last, with a Bull Market and a system of Pyramids, he began to sweep it in with his Fore-Arm.

Head Waiters paid him the most grovelling Attentions and bright eyes grew brighter yet when he suggested pulling a little Supper, with a $400 Souvenir at each Plate.

He was admitted to full membership in the Tango Tribe of the Tenderloin Night-Riders.

This select Coterie was organized for the purpose of closing all Cabarets by 6 A. M..

An early hour was named because many of them were not made up for the cold Daylight.

About the time he began to discover Vintages he discovered Elphye also. She was an Actress who was too busy to perform on the Stage.

Elphye had a good Social Position back at her Home lot but, for some reason, she never sent for it.

Her Parents had arranged for her to be a Brunette, but when Bob met her, between the Guinea Hen and the Cafe Parfait, she was a Lemon Meringue.

Elphye wore Clothes that made a noise like a Piccolo.

She was there with the jeweled Heels and the hand-painted Ankles.

In trying to make her Gowns anywhere from six to nine months ahead of Paris, she sprung several Effects that caused the Chandeliers to tremble and the Ice to melt in the Buckets.

She had abolished her Shape entirely and abandoned the Perpendicular, preferring a Droop which indicated that possibly she had been fashioned over a Barrel.

She tried to model herself on the lines of a string Bean, slightly warped by the Sun.

The Ascending Star of the Financial World was stunned by the Apparition. No one had tipped it off to him that the Queen of Sheba was to be reincarnated.

He found Elphye ever and ever so accomplished.

She knew all the Songs that now blister the Varnish off the Pianos in so many well-ordered Homes.

She was enough of a Contortionist to get away with several Dances named for the innocent Poultry.

Being a close student of the Bill-Boards she was in touch with Current Happenings.

Her Eye-Work was perfect, but she found it hard pumping to Blush at the right time.

When she tackled Polite Conversation she put a few Tooth-Marks in it.

Still she made a very creditable Stab for a Girl brought up in Michigan and never east of Sheepshead Bay.

She looked very creamy to Bob, if the Music was loud enough.

He liked to tow something that would cause the Oyster Forks to pause in midair and the Catty Ones to reach for their hardware.

When Elphye did a little Barnum and Bailey down the main Chute of a Terrapin Bazaar, rest assured that every Eye in the Resort was aimed at her gleaming Vertebrae.

Bob showed her his monthly Statements and she confessed to being very fond of him. So it was planned that they would Marry some afternoon, if she could get away from the Masseuse early enough.

The Troth was pledged in a few high-priced Trinkets which she had decided upon before he spoke to her.

Just when it seemed a mortal Pipe that the Bull Tactics would enable him to cop a Million, so that he could live at a Hotel and finance the Little Queen, the Unseen Superintendent in the Tower began to throw the Switches of Destiny.

If Bob had not speeded so far into the Country in the Smell-Wagon, there would have been no Flat Tire.

If there had been no Flat Tire, he would have been back in time for the usual round-up of the Irrigation Committee and never would have been a Great Financier.

Marooned among the Hay-Fields, he stopped at a Farm House and took a long chance on some Well-Water, dipped in a Gourd from the Moss-Covered Bucket.

Scotch Whiskey is never contaminated by Surface Drains, but each sparkling Drop of the Fluid that Bob quaffed, there beneath the Willows, contained more than 2,000,000 of the Germs made notorious by Dr. Woods Hutchinson.

A few days later a swarm of Bees settled in each ear. Every Sky-Scraper gave an imitation of the Leaning Tower of Pisa.

He knew he was out of Kelter, but he had to watch the Board, for he had put every Bean in the World on an acrobatic Industrial known as Tin Bucket Preferred.

Already the Paper Profits were enormous. Bob figured confidently on another Whoop of 50 points and a double string of Pearls for Elphye. But when the poor Loon had a Temperature of 5 above Par and had to cling to the Brass Rail to keep from taking the Count, he lost his Nerve entirely.

He couldn't see anything on the Horizon except Tariff Revision, Hard Times, Weeping Women, Starving Kiddies, Closed Factories, Soup Kitchens, and Bread Lines.

While in this dotty State and quite irresponsible, he directed the Manager to close out the whole Smear and sell short.

Furthermore, he was so daffy and curdled in the Filbert that he sold three times as much as he had.

Then he did a couple of Spins and a Flop, and the White Ambulance bore him away to the big Hospital.

If Mr. Hornung Jackson of Round Grove, Maryland, had not entered upon his Second Childhood at the age of 55, his Family would have remained on Easy Street.

Mr. Jackson thought he could sit in his Front Room and read the burglarious Meditations of the High-Binders in Wall Street.

Consequently, when the Tin Box was searched, the Day after the Masons had marched out to the Cemetery, it contained a little of everything except Assets.

Annie was the name of the Daughter.

On the Clean-up she received enough to put her through the School.

When Bob arrived at the Hospital, in a State of Conflagration, Annie was waiting in the starched Uniform to tackle her first real Case.

For days and nights he rambled through the ghostly labyrinths of Delirium, Annie holding him by the Hand and lifting the cool Draughts to his parched Lips.

He mumbled and raved about the decisions of the Umpire in the game between the Academy and the Knitting Works.

He gave Annie his entire performance of Ralph Rackstraw in "Pinafore" for the benefit of the Library Fund, including Cues.

He scolded his Aunt Mary for doing her own Housework and told the Colored Men how to lay the Cement Walk down through the Grape Arbor. He promised his Father not to play Poker any more and vowed to his Mother that she was a better Chef than the one up at Del's. But his sub-conscious Self was so considerate of Elphye that he never brought in her Name at all, at all.

Sometimes he would get back to the Ticker, but he was ready to leave it any time to go fishing in the Crick with the Lads from the other side of the Tracks.

Through the final Crisis he played tag with the Grim Reaper and just escaped being It.

The Sun was slanting into the little white Room when he crawled feebly back to Earth and tried to get his Bearings.

Annie was looking right at him, relieved and smiling and happy. She had won her first game in the Big League.

He noticed that she was not slashed up the side or down the back, had no metallic Insteps, carried her own Hair, and was in no way concealed behind the usual pallid Veneering.

He remembered dimly that she had been with him on the Underground.

Then he recalled a previous Existence in which the Dripped

Absinthe was a Breakfast and the Cigarette a Luncheon and Elphye was trotting in her Glads and he had a Swell Bet down on Tin Bucket Preferred. The whole Lay-Out seemed unreal and remote and entirely disconnected with Friend Nurse.

He inquired the Day of the Week, and when he learned it was Next Month he started to get right up and put on his Things.

Annie quietly spread him back on the Pillow and laid down the Law regarding Rest and Quiet.

Then he begged her to ring up McCusick & Co. and get the latest Bucket Preferred.

He said he had plastered his last Samoelon and, not being there to watch the Board and concentrate his wonderful Trading Instinct on every jiggle of the Dial, there was no telling what the Bone-Heads had done to him.

You see, he had no recollection whatever of going Short, for he had been in a Walking Delirium at the time and crazy as a Cubist.

Annie said it was wrong to Gamble and he was not to read the Papers or fuss with Visitors until Doc gave the word.

Suddenly he remembered that he was engaged to Elphye and he wondered if she had forgotten.

So many things can happen in a Great City within two weeks.

He told Nurse about Elphye. Annie did not seem madly interested, but she wrote a Note to the Sazerack Apartment Building and notified the Seraphine that her prospective Producer was still extant and would be willing to renew acquaintance if she could spare an hour or two from her Dancing.

Elphye came out two days later made up as a Princess in the Christmas Pantomime and diffusing pleasant Odors in all directions.

She sat down alongside of Annie and immediately she was shown up and went back to the Minors.

Her Second-Reader Conversation, complicated with the phoney Boston sound of "A" as in "Squash," did not improve her General Average. Bob suddenly realized that in getting rid of the Bronxes and the Nicotine and various other Toxins, he also had lost his appetite for Elphye.

But he was Game and willing to go through on his own Proposition. He sent Nurse for a glass of Water and then begged his Fiancee to smuggle in a Newspaper so he could find out the name of his getting-off Station.

Next day she brought the Market Page in her wonderful jewel-crusted Bag. Bob took one Look and crawled under the Covers.

The Market had gone Blooey.

Bucket Preferred was down in the Subway, bleeding from a dozen Wounds. The Whole List was on the Blinkety Fritz.

"Courage, Dearie," said Bob, taking Elphye by the Rings. "Your little Playmate is erased from the map."

Elphye upset two Rolling Chairs and one Interne getting from the Convalescent Department to the open Air.

Annie found the poor Bankrupt much improved as to Pulse and Temperature. He told her the whole Story of how his Lady Fair had canned him because he was no longer a Live One.

She held his hand and pushed back his Locks and told him that any Girl with a Heart would stick closer than ever to her Selection when he was under the Rollers.

Just then a Messenger from McCusick came in and showed Bob that by going Short and standing pat he was $1,800,000 to the Desirable. After that, Bob was known up and down the Street as The Wizard.

Annabelle, remembering how they had got to her Father, made him cut out the Margins and put the whole Chunk into listed Securities and Real Estate.

He wanted to stick around and parlee up to a Billion, but she raised a most emphatic Nixey.

He was so used to taking orders from her as a Trained Nurse that he cut out speculating and played Safe.

The whole game was punk for months after, so every one said he had been a Wise Mug for backing away.

The Missus allows him a light one (mostly Vermouth) before Dinner each evening and has taught him a private Signal which means that she is ready to duck and go Home.

At present they are in Paris, where she is working to get the same hilarious *Tout Ensemble* formerly exhibited by Elphye, the Ex-Empress of the White Light Reservation.

The latter went to see a Lawyer when she learned that she had been tricked out of her Happiness.

Unfortunately for her, she had nothing on Robert, thanks to his native shrewdness and Mr. Bell, who invented the Telephone.

She is now playing Utility Parts in a Stock Company in Pennsylvania. The Jewels pelted at her by Bob are much admired by the Gallery.

MORAL: The City holds no Peril for those who cherish Lucky Ideals.

THE NEW FABLE OF SUSAN AND THE DAUGHTER AND THE GRAND-DAUGHTER, AND THEN SOMETHING REALLY GRAND

Once there was a full-blown Wild Peach, registered in the Family Bible as Susan Mahaly.

Her Pap divided his time between collecting at a Toll-Gate and defending the Military Reputation of Andy Jackson.

The family dwelt in what was then regarded by Cambridge, Mass., as the Twilight Zone of Semi-Culture, viz., Swigget County, Pennsylvania. Susan wore Linsey-Woolsey from Monday to Saturday. She never had tampered with her Venus de Milo Topography and she did not even suspect that Women had Nerves.

When she was seventeen she had a Fore-Arm like a Member of the Turnverein.

She knew how to Card and Weave and Dye. Also she could make Loose Soap in a kettle out in the Open Air.

Susan never fell down on her Salt-Rising Bread. Her Apple Butter was always A1.

It was commonly agreed that she would make some Man a good Housekeeper, for she was never sickly and could stay on her Feet sixteen hours at a Stretch.

George Ade

Already she was beginning to look down the Pike for a regular Fellow. In the year 1840, the Lass of seventeen who failed to get her Hooks on some roaming specimen of the Opposite Gender was in danger of being whispered about as an Old Maid. Celibacy was listed with Arson and Manslaughter.

Rufus was destined to be an Early Victorian Rummy, but he could lift a Saw-Log, and he would stand without being hitched, so Susan nailed him the third time he came snooping around the Toll-Gate.

Rufus did not have a Window to hoist or a Fence to lean on. But there is no Poverty in any Pocket of the Universe until Wealth arrives and begins to get Luggy.

Susan thought she was playing in rare Luck to snare a Six-Footer who owned a good Squirrel Rifle and could out-wrastle all Comers.

The Hills of Pennsylvania were becoming congested, with Neighbors not more than two or three miles apart, so Rufus and his Bride decided to hit a New Trail into the Dark Timber and grow up with the Boundless West.

Relatives of the Young Couple staked them to a team of Pelters, a Muley Cow, a Bird Dog of dubious Ancestry, an Axe and a Skillet, and started them over the Divide toward the perilous Frontier, away out yender in Illinoy.

It was a Hard Life. As they trundled slowly over the rotten Roads, toward the Land of Promise, they had to subsist largely on Venison, Prairie Chicken, Quail, Black Bass, Berries, and Wild Honey. They carried their own Coffee.

Arrived at the Jumping-Off Place, they settled down among the Mink and Musk-Rats. Rufus hewed out and jammed together a little two by twice Cabin with the Flue running up the outside. It looked ornery enough to be the Birthplace of almost any successful American.

The Malaria Mosquito was waiting for the Pioneers. In those good old Chills-and-Fever days, no one ever blamed it on the Female of the Species. Those who had the Shakes allowed that they were being jarred by the Hand of Providence.

When the family ran low on Quinine, all he had to do was hook up and drive fifty miles to the nearest Town, where he would trade the Furs for Necessities such as Apple-Jack and Navy Twist, and possibly a few Luxuries such as Tea and Salt.

On one of these memorable Trips to the Store, a Mood which combined Sentiment with reckless Prodigality seized upon him.

He thought of the brave Woman who was back there in the lonesome Shack, shooing the Prairie Wolves away from the Cradle, and he resolved to reward her.

With only three Gills of Stone Fence under his Wammus, he spread his Wild-Cat Currency on the Counter and purchased a $6 Clock, with jig-saw ornaments, a shiny coat of Varnish, and a Bouquet of Pink Roses on the door.

Susan burst into Tears when she saw it on the Wall, alongside of the Turkey Wing, and vowed that she had married the Best Man in the World.

Twenty years later, Jennie, the first begotten Chick at the Log House in the Clearing, had matured and married, and was living at the County-Seat with Hiram, Money-Changer and Merchant.

Railroad Trains, Side-Bar Buggies, Coal-Oil Lamps, and the Civil War had come along with a Rush and disarranged primitive Conditions. The Frontier had retreated away over into Kansas.

In the very Township where, of late, the Beaver had toiled without Hindrance and the Red Fox dug his hole unscared, people were now eating Cove Oysters, and going to see "East Lynne."

Hiram was in rugged Health, having defended the flag by Proxy during the recent outcropping of Acrimony between the devotees of Cold Bread and the slaves of Hot Biscuit. The Substitute had been perforated beyond repair at the Battle of Kennesaw Mountain, proving that Hiram made no mistake in remaining behind to tend Store.

When Jennie moved in where she could hear the Trains whistle and began to sport a Cameo Brooch, she could barely remember wearing a Slip and having Stone Bruises.

Hiram was Near, but he would Loosen up a trifle for his own Fireside. The fact that Jennie was his wife gave her quite a Standing with him. He admired her for having made such a Success of her Life.

They dwelt in a two-story Frame with countless Dewdads and Thingumbobs tacked along the Eaves and Scalloped around the Bay Windows.

The Country People who came in to see the Eighth Wonder of the World used to stand in silent Awe, breathing through their Noses.

Out on the lawn, surrounded by Geraniums, was a Cast-Iron Deer which seemed to be looking at the Court House in a startled Manner. It was that kind of a Court House.

In her Front Room, the daughter of Rufus and Susan had Wonderful Wax Flowers, sprinkled with Diamond Dust; a What-Not bearing Mineral Specimens, Conch-Shells, and a Star-Fish, also some Hair-Cloth Furniture, very slippery and upholstered with Sand.

After Hiram gave her the Black Silk and paid for the Crayon Enlargements of her Parents, Jennie did not have the Face to bone him for anything more, but she longed in secret and Hiram suspected. Jennie was a soprano. Not a regular Soprano, but a Country-Town Soprano, of the kind often used for augmenting the Grief in a Funeral. Her voice came from a point about two inches above the Right Eye. She had assisted a Quartette to do things to "Juanita," and sometimes tossed out little Hints about wishing she could practice at Home. Jennie was a Nice Woman but she *did* need Practice.

Although Hiram was tighter than the Bark on a Sycamore, he liked to have other Women envy the Mother of His Children.

When he spread himself from a Shin-Plaster, he expected a Fanfare of Trumpets.

It took him a long time to unwind the String from the Wallet, but he would Dig if he thought he was boosting his own Game.

By stealthy short-weighting of the Country Trade and holding out on the Assessor, he succeeded in salting away numerous Kopecks in one corner of the Safe.

While in Chicago to buy his Winter Stock, he bargained for two days and finally bought a Cottage Melodeon, with the Stool thrown in.

Jennie would sit up and pump for Hours at a time, happy in the knowledge that she had drawn the Capital Prize in the Lottery of Hymen.

In the year 1886 there was some Church Wedding at the County Seat. Frances, daughter of Hiram and Jennie, had knocked the Town a Twister when she came home from the Female College wearing Bangs and toting a Tennis Racquet.

All the local Gallants, with Cocoa-Oil in their hair and Rings on their Cravats, backed into the Shrubbery.

Hiram had bought her about $1800 worth of Hauteur at the select Institution of Learning. All she had to do was look at a Villager through her Nose-Specs and he would curl up like an Autumn Leaf.

A Cuss from Chicago came to see her every two weeks.

His Trousers seemed to be choking him. The Pompadour was protected by a Derby of the Fried-Egg species. It was the kind that Joe Weber helped to keep in Public Remembrance. But in 1886 it was de Rigeur, au Fait, and a la mode.

Frances would load the hateful City Chap into the high Cart and exhibit him up and down all the Residence Thorough-fares.

On nearly every Front Porch some Girl whose Father was not interested in the First National Bank would peer out through the Morning Glories at the Show-off and then writhe like an Angle-Worm.

The Wedding was the biggest thing that had struck the town since Forepaugh stopped over on his way from Peoria to Decatur.

Frances was not a popular Girl, on account of being so Uppish, so those who could not fight their way into the Church climbed up and looked through the Windows.

The Groom wore a Swallow-Tail.

Most of those present had seen Pictures of the Dress Suit. In the *Fireside Companion,* the Gentleman wearing one always had Curls, and the Wood-Engraving caught him in the act of striking a Lady in the Face and saying "Curse you!"

The Feeling at the County-Seat was that Frances had taken a Desperate Chance.

The caterer with Colored Help in White Gloves, the ruby Punch suspected of containing Liquor, the Japanese Lanterns attached to the Maples, the real Lace in the Veil, the glittering Array of Pickle-Jars, and a well-defined Rumor that most of the imported Ushers had been Stewed, gave the agitated Hamlet something to blat about for many and many a day.

The Bachelor of Arts grabbed off by the daughter of Jennie and the Grand-daughter of Susan was the owner of Real Estate in the congested Business District of a Town which came into Public Attention later on through the efforts of Frank Chance.

His front name was Willoughby, but Frances always called him "Dear," no matter what she happened to be thinking of at the time.

Part of State Street had been wished on to Willoughby. He was afraid to sell, not knowing how to reinvest.

So he sat back and played safe. With growing Delight he watched the Unearned Increment piling up on every Corner. He began to see that he would be fairly busy all his life, jacking up Rents.

The Red-Brick Fortress to which he conducted Frances had Stone Steps in front and a secret Entrance for lowly Tradespeople at the rear.

Willoughby and his wife had the high courage of Youth and the Financial Support of all the Money Spenders along State Street, so they started in on Period Decoration. Each Room in the House was supposed to stand for a Period. Some of them stood for a great deal.

A few of the Periods looked like Exclamation Points.

The young couple disregarded the Toll-Gate Period and the Log-Cabin Period, but they worked in every one of the Louies until the Gilt Furniture gave out.

The delighted Caller at the House beside the Lake would pass from an East Indian Corridor through an Early Colonial American Room into a Japanese Boudoir and, after resting his Hat, would be escorted into the Italian Renaissance Drawing-Room to meet the Hostess. From this exquisite Apartment, which ate up one year's Rent of a popular Buffet near Van Buren Street, there could be obtained a ravishing glimpse of the Turkish Cozy Corner beyond, including the Battle-Axes and the Red Lamp.

Frances soon began to hob-nob with the most delicatessen Circles, including Families that dated back to the Fire of 1871.

She was not at all Dizzy, even when she looked down from the Mountain Peak at her happy Birthplace, 15,000 feet below.

Willoughby turned out to be a satisfactory Housemate. His Voltage was not high, but he always ate Peas with a Fork and never pulled at the Leash when taken to a Musicale.

In front of each Ear he carried a neat Area of Human Ivy, so that he could speak up at a Meeting of Directors. Until the year 1895, the restricted Side-Whisker was an accepted Trade-Mark of Commercial Probity. This facial Landscaping, the Frock Coat, and a steadfast devotion to Toilet Soap made him suitable for Exhibition Purposes.

Frances became almost fond of him, after the Honeymoon evaporated and their Romance ripened into Acquaintanceship.

It was a gladsome day for both when she traced the Dope back through Swigget County, Pennsylvania, and discovered that she was an honest-to-goodness Daughter of the American Revolution.

Willoughby could not ask a representative of good old Colonial Stock to ride around in a stingy Coupe with a Coon planted out on the Weather-Seat.

He changed the Terms in several Leases and was enabled to slip her a hot Surprise on the Birthday.

When she came down the Steps for the usual bowl along the Avenue, so as to get some Fresh Smoke, she beheld a rubber-tired Victoria, drawn by two expensive Bang-Tails in jingly Harness and surmounted by important Turks in overwhelming Livery.

She was so trancified with Delight that she went right over to Willoughby and gave him a Sweet Kiss, after looking about rather carefully for the exposed portion of the Frontispiece.

Frances did a lot of Calling within the next two weeks, and to all those who remarked upon the Smartness of the Equipage, she declared that the Man she had to put up with carried a Throbbing Heart even if he was an Intellectual Midget.

In the year 1913, a slender Young Thing, all of whose Habiliments seemed melting and dripping downward, came wearily from Stateroom B as the Train pulled into Reno, Nevada.

She seemed quite alone, except for a couple of Maids.

After she had given Directions concerning the nine Wardrobe Trunks and the Live Stock, she was motored to a specially reserved Cottage at the corner of Liberty Street and Hope Avenue.

Next day she sat at the other side of a Table from a Lawyer, removing the poisoned Javelins from her fragile Person and holding them up before the shuddering Shyster.

She had a Tale of Woe calculated to pulp a Heart of Stone. In blocking out the Affidavit, her sympathetic Attorney made Pencil Notes as follows:

Her name was Ethel Louise, favorite Daughter of Willoughby

and Frances, the well-known Blue-Bloods of the Western Metropolis.

She had finished off at Miss Sniffle's exclusive School, which overlooks the Hudson and the Common School Branches.

After she learned to enter a Ball-Room and while on her way to attack Europe for the third time, the Viper crossed her Pathway.

She accepted him because his name was Hubert, he looked like an Englishman, and one of his Ancestors turned the water into Chesapeake Bay.

While some of the Wedding Guests were still in the Hospital, he began to practice the most diabolical Cruelties.

He induced her to get on his Yacht and go cruising through the Mediterranean when she wanted to take an Apartment in Paris.

At Monte Carlo he scolded her for borrowing 3000 Francs from a Russian Grand Duke after she went broke at bucking the Wheel. She had met the Duke at a Luncheon the day before and his Manners were perfect.

The Lawyer said that Herbert was a Pup, beyond all Cavil.

Cairo, Egypt, yielded up another Dark Chapter of History.

It came out in the sobbing Recital that Hubert had presented her with a $900 prize-winning Pomeranian, directly related to the famous Fifi, owned by the Countess Skidoogan of Bilcarty.

Later on, he seemed to feel that the Pomeranian had come between him and Ethel. The Situation became more and more tense, and finally, one day in Egypt, within plain sight of the majestic Pyramids, he kicked Precious ever so hard and raised quite a Swelling.

The Legal Adviser said Death was too good for such a Fiend.

In Vienna, though, that was where he went so far that Separation became inevitable.

Ethel had decided to take an $80,000 Pearl Necklace she had seen in a Window. It was easily worth that much, and she felt sure she could get it in without paying Duty. She had been very successful at bringing things Home.

She could hardly believe her Ears when Hubert told her to forget it and back up and come out of the Spirit World and alight on the Planet Earth. He had been Heartless on previous Occasions, but this was the first time he had been Mean enough to renig on a mere side-issue such as coming across with the Loose Change.

Ethel was simply de-termined to have that Necklace, but the unfeeling Whelp tried to kid her out of the Notion.

Then he started in to Pike. He suggested a $20,000 Tarara of Rubies and Diamonds as a Compromise. Ethel became wise to the fact that she had joined out with a Wad.

While she was pulling a daily Sick Headache in the hope of bringing him to Taw, the Maharajah of Umslopagus came along and bought the Necklace. That was when Ethel had to be taken to a Rest Cure in the Austrian Tyrol, and she had never been the Same Woman since.

To all who had come pleading for Reconciliation, Ethel had simply hung out the Card, "Nothing Doing."

After a Brute has jumped up and down on the Aching Heart of a Girl of proud Lineage he can't square himself in 1,000,000 years.

So said Ethel, between the flowing Tears.

Furthermore, there had been hopeless Incompatibility. In all the time they were together, they never had been able to agree on a Turkish Cigarette.

The professional Home-Blaster said she had enough on Herbert to get her four Divorces. The Decree would be a Pipe.

Ethel said she hoped so and to please push it along, as she had quite a Waiting-List.

MORAL: Rufus had no business buying the Clock.

THE NEW FABLE OF THE SCOFFER WHO FELL HARD AND THE WOMAN SITTING BY

One day in the pink dawn of the present Century, a man with his Hair neatly set back around the Ears and the usual Blood Pressure was whizzing through a suburban Lonesomeness on a teetering Trolley. The name of the man was Mr. Pallzey. He had a desk with a Concern that did merchandizing in a large way.

Mr. Pallzey feared Socialism and carried his Wife's Picture in his Watch and wore Plasters. In other words, he was Normal, believing nearly everything that appeared in the Papers.

While the Dog-Fennel was softly brushing the Foot-Board and the Motor was purring consistently beneath, Mr. Pallzey looked over into a close-cropped Pasture and became the alert Eye-Witness of some very weird Doings.

He saw a pop-eyed Person in soiled Neglige, who made threatening movements toward something concealed in the White Clover, with a Weapon resembling the iron Dingus used in gouging the Clinkers from a Furnace.

"What is the plot of the Piece?" he inquired of a Grand Army man, sitting next.

"I think," replied the Veteran, "I think he is killing a Garter Snake."

"Oh, no," spoke up the conversational Conductor, "He is playing Golluf," giving the word the Terre Haute pronunciation.

Mr. Pallzey looked with pity on the poor Nut who was out in the Hot Sun, getting himself all lathered up with One-Man Shinny.

He said to G. A. R. that it took all kinds of People to make a World. The grizzled Warrior rose to an equal Altitude by remarking that if the dag-goned Loon had to do it for a Living, he'd think it was Work. Mr. Pallzey had heard of the new Diversion for the Idle Rich, just as people out in the Country hear of Milk-Sickness or falling Meteors, both well authenticated but never encountered.

While rummaging through the Sporting Page, he would come across a cryptic Reference to MacFearson of Drumtochtie being 3 up and 2 to play on Hargis of Sunset Ho, whereupon he would experience a sense of annoyance and do a quick Hurdle.

He had seen in various Shop-Windows the spindly Utensils and snowy Pellets which, he had reason to believe, were affiliated in some way with the sickening Fad. He would look at them with extreme Contempt and rather resent their contaminating contiguity to the Mask , the Shin-Guard, and the upholstered Grabber.

Mr. Pallzey believed that Golf was played by the kind of White Rabbits who March in Suffrage Parades, wearing Gloves.

The dreaded Thing lay outside of his Orbit and beyond his Ken, the same as Tatting or Biology. His conception of a keen and sporty game was Pin Pool or Jacks Only with the Deuce running wild.

One Saturday he was invited out to a Food Saturnalia at a Country Place. The Dinner was postponed until late in the

Day because they all dreaded it so much.

Friend Host said he had a twosome on at the Club and was trying out an imported Cleek, so he invited Mr. Pallzey to be a Spectator.

If he had said that he was going up in a Balloon to hemstitch a coupleof Clouds, it would have sounded just as plausible to Mr. Pallzey of the Wholesale District.

The latter went along, just out of Politeness, but he was a good deal disappointed in his Friend. It certainly did seem trifling for a Huskie weighing one hundred and eighty to pick on something about the size of a Robin's Egg.

Mr. Pallzey played Gallery all around the Course. He would stand behind them at the Tee and smile in a most calm and superior Manner while they sand-shuffled and shifted and jiggled and joggledand went through the whole calisthenic Ritual of St. Vitus.

He was surprised to note how far the Ball would speed when properly spanked, but he thought there was no valid excuse for overrunning on the Approaches.

Mr. Pallzey found himself criticizing the Form of the Players. That should have been his Cue to climb the Fence.

All of the Mashiemaniacs start on the downward Path by making Mind-Plays and getting under Bogey.

Back on the sloping Sward between No. 18 and the Life-Saving Station, the two Contestants were holding the usual Post-Mortem.

"Let me see that Dewflicker a minute," said Mr. Pallzey, as he carelessly extracted a Mid-iron.

He sauntered up to the silly Globule and took an

unpremeditated Swipe. The Stroke rang sweet and vibrant. The ball rose in parabolic Splendor above the highest branches of a venerable Elm.

Just as the Face of the Club started on the Follow Through, the Bacillus ran up and bit Mr. Pallzey on the Leg.

He saw the blinking White Spot far out on the emerald Plain. He heard the murmur of Admiration behind him. He was sorry his Wife had not been there to take it in.

"Leave me have another Ball," requested Mr. Pallzey.

The Virus was working.

He backed up so as to get a Running Start.

"This time," quoth Mr. Pallzey, "I will push it to Milwaukee."

Missing the Object of Attack by a scant six inches, he did a Genee toe-spin and fell heavily with his Face among the Dandelions.

The Host brushed him off and said: "Your Stance was wrong; your Tee was too high; you raised the Left Shoulder; you were too rapid on the Come-Back; the Grip was all in the Left Hand; you looked up; you moved your Head at the top of the Stroke; you allowed the Left Knee to turn, and you stood ahead of the Ball. Otherwise, it was a Loo-Loo."

"If I come out next Sunday could you borrow me a Kit of Tools?" asked Mr. Pallzey. He was twitching violently and looking at the Ball as if it had called him a Name. "I got that first one all right, and I think—"

So it was arranged that the poor doomed Creature was to appear on the following Sabbath and be equipped with a set of Cast-Offs and learn all about the Mystery of the Ages between

11 A. M. and 2 P. M..

Mr. Pallzey went away not knowing that he was a Marked Man.

On Monday he told the Stenographer how he stung the Ball the first time up. He said he was naturally quick at picking up any kind of Game. He thought it would be a Lark to get the hang of the Whole Business and then get after some of those Berties in the White Pants. He figured that Golf would be soft for any one who had played Baseball when young. Truly all the raving is not done within the Padded Cells.

He came home in the Sabbath Twilight, walking on his Ankles and babbling about a Dandy Drive for the Long Hole.

Regarding the other 378 Strokes he was discreetly silent.

He told his Wife there was more in it than one would suppose. The Easier the Swat, the greater the Carry. And he had made one Hole in seven.

Then he took a Parasol out of the Jar, and illustrated the famous Long Drive with Moving Pictures, Tableaux, Delsarte, and some newly acquired technical Drivel, which he mouthed with childish Delight.

Now we see him buying Clubs, although he refers to them as Sticks—proving that he is still a groping Neophyte.

He thinks that a shorter Shaft and more of a Lay-Back will enable him to drive a Mile. The Gooseneck Putter will save him two on every Hole. Also, will the Man please show him an Iron guaranteed to reach all the way down to the Dimple and plunk it right in the Eye.

Then all of the new Implements laid out at Home and Wife sitting back, listening to a Lecture as to what will be pulled off on the succeeding Day of Rest.

She had promised at the Altar to Love, Honor, and Listen. Still, it was trying to see the once-loved Adult cavorting on the verge of Dementia and know that she was helpless.

He sallied forth with those going to Early Mass, and returned at the Vesper Hour caked with Dust and 98 per cent. gone in the Turret.

It seems that at the sixth hole on the Last Round where you cross the Crick twice, he fell down and broke both Arms and both Legs. So he tore up the Medal Score, gave all the Clubs to the Caddy, and standing on the grassy Summit of the tall Ridge guarding the Bunker, he had lifted a grimy Paw and uttered the Vow of Renunciation.

In other words, he was Through.

The senile Wrecks and the prattling Juveniles, for whom the Game was invented, could have his Part of it for all time.

Never again would he walk on the Grass or cock his Arms or dribble Sand all over the dark and trampled Ground where countless Good Men had suffered.

No, Indeed!

So next day he bought all the Paraphernalia known to the Trade, and his name was put up at a Club.

It was one of those regular and sure-enough Clubs. High East Winds prevailed in the Locker-Room. Every member was a Chick Evans when he got back to the nineteenth hole.

Mr. Pallzey now began to regard the Ancient and Honorable Pastime as a compendium of Sacraments, Ordeals, Incantations, and Ceremonial Formalities.

He resigned himself into the Custody of a professional Laddie with large staring Knuckles and a Dialect that dimmed all the memories of Lauder.

In a short time the Form was classy, but the Score had to be taken out and buried after every Round.

Mr. Pallzey saw that this Mundane Existence was not all Pleasure. He had found his Life-Work. The Lode-Star of his declining Years would be an even one hundred for the eighteen Flags.

Wife would see him out in the Street, feeling his way along, totally unmindful of his Whereabouts. She would lead him into the Shade, snap her Fingers, call his Name, and gradually pull him out of the Trance. He would look at her with a filmy Gaze and smile faintly, as if partly remembering and then say: "Don't forget to follow through. Keep the head down—tight with the left—no hunching—pivot on the hips. For a Cuppy Lie, take the Nib. If running up with the Jigger, drop her dead. The full St. Andrews should not be thrown into a Putt. Never up, never in. Lift the flag. Take a pickout from Casual Water but play the Road-ways. To overcome Slicing or Pulling, advance the right or left Foot. Schlaffing and Socketing may be avoided by adding a hook with top-spin or *vice versa*. The Man says there are twenty-six Things to be remembered in Driving from the Tee. One is Stance. I forget the other twenty-five."

Then the Partner of his Joys and Sorrows, with the accent on the Debit Side, would shoot twenty Grains of Asperin into him and plant him in the Flax.

Next morning at Breakfast he would break it to her that the Brassie had developed too much of a Whip and he had decided to try a forty-inch Shaft.

They had Seasoned Hickory for Breakfast, Bunkers for Luncheon, and the Fair Green for Dinner.

As a matter of course they had to give up their comfortable Home among the Friends who had got used to them and move out to a strawboard Bungalow so as to be near the Execution Grounds.

Mrs. Pallzey wanted to do the White Mountains, but Mr. Pallzey needed her. He wanted her to be waiting on the Veranda at Dusk, so that he could tell her all about it, from the preliminary Address to the final Foozle.

Sometimes he would come home enveloped in a foglike Silence which would last beyond early Candle Lighting, when he would express the Opinion that the Administration at Washington had proved a Failure.

Perhaps the very next Evening he would lope all the way up the Gravel and breeze into her presence, smelling like a warm gust of Air from Dundee.

He would ask her to throw an Amber Light on the Big Hero. He would call her "Kid" and say that Vardon had nothing on him. Her man was the Gink to show that Pill how to take a Joke.

Then she would know that he had won a Box of Balls from Mrs. Talbot's poor old crippled Father-in-Law.

She could read him like a Barometer. If he and Mr. Hilgus, the Real Estate Man, came home together fifteen feet apart, she would know it had been a Jolly Day on the Links.

By the second summer, Mr. Pallzey had worked up until he was allowed to use a Shower Bath once hallowed by the presence of Jerome Travers.

He was not exactly a Duffer. He was what might be called a sub-Duffer, or Varnish, which means that the Committee was ashamed to mark up the Handicap.

He still had a good many superfluous Hands and Feet and was bleeding freely on every Green.

Sometimes he would last as far as the Water-Hazard and then sink with a Bubbling Cry.

Notwithstanding which, he kept on trying to look like the Photographs of Ouimet.

If he spun into the High Spinach off at the Right it was Tough Luck. If he whanged away with a Niblick down in a bottomless Pit, caromed on a couple of Oaks, and finally angled off toward the Cup, he would go around for Days talking about Some Shot.

As his Ambition increased, his Mental Arithmetic became more and more defective and his Moral Nature was wholly atrophied.

As an Exponent of the more advanced Play he was a Fliv, but as a Matchmaker he was a Hum-Dinger.

He knew he was plain pastry for the Sharks, so he would hang around the first Tee waiting to cop out a Pudding.

One day he took on Mrs. Olmstead's Infant Son, just home from Military School.

The tender Cadet nursed him along to an even-up at the Punch-Bowl and then proceeded to smear his vital Organs all over the Bad Lands.

That evening Mr. Pallzey told her she would have to cut down on Household Expenses.

Six years after he gave up the Business Career and consecrated himself to something more Important, Mr. Pallzey had so well mastered the baffling Intricacies that he was allowed to trail in a Foursome with the President of the Club. This happened once.

It is well known that any Person who mooches around a

Country Club for a sufficient Period will have some kind of a Cup wished on to him. Fourteen years after Mr. Pallzey threw himself into it, Heart and Soul, and when the Expenses approximated $30,000, he earned his Halo.

One evening he came back to his haggard Companion, chortling infant-wise, and displayed something which looked like an Eye-Cup with Handles on it.

He said it was a Trophy. It was a Consolation Offering for Maidens with an allowance of more than eighteen.

After that their daily Life revolved around the $2 bargain in Britannia. Mrs. Pallzey had to use Metal Polish on it to keep it from turning black.

When the Visitors lined up in front of the Mantel and gazed at the tiny Shaving Mug, the Cellar Champion on the World would regale them with the story of hairbreadth 'Scapes and moving Adventures by Gravel Gullies and rushing Streams on the Memorable Day when he (Pallzey) had put the Blocks to Old Man McLaughlin, since deceased.

Then he would ask all present to feel of his Forearm, after which he would pull the Favorite One about Golf adding ten years to his life.

Mrs. Pallzey would be sitting back, pouring Tea, but she never chimed in with any Estimate as to what had been the effect on her Table of Expectations.

MORAL: Remain under the Awning.

THE NEW FABLE OF THE LONESOME CAMP ON THE FROZEN HEIGHTS

Elam was the main Whizzer in a huddle of Queen Annes, bounded on the North by a gleaming Cemetery, on the East by a limping subdivision, on the South by a deserted Creamery, and on the West by an expanse of Stubble.

Claudine was the other two-thirds of the Specialty.

She was a snappy little Trick and it was a dull hour of the Day or Night when she couldn't frame up a new General Order for the Breadwinner.

The Marriage came off during the third summer of her twenty-seventh year.

She accepted Elam about a week before he proposed to her, thus simplifying the Ordeal.

While the Wafer on the License was still warm, she put on her spangled Suit, moved to the centre of the Ring, and cracked the Whip.

After than Elam continued to be a Hellion around the Office, but in his private Quarters he was merely Otto, the Trained Seal.

Claudine could make him Bark, play the Cymbals, or go back to the Blue Bench.

There is one Elam in every Settlement.

All the wise Paper-hangers and the fly Guitar Players had him marked up as a Noodle, but somehow, every time the winning Numbers were hung out, he would be found in Line, waiting to Cash.

He was not Bright enough to do anything except garner the Gold Certificates.

Elam had no Ear for Music, and, coming out of the Opera House, never could remember the name of the Play or which one of the Burglars was the real Hero.

His Reading was confined to the Headlines of a conservative Paper which was still printing War News.

Baseball had not come into his Life whatsoever.

A cultured Steno, who knew about George Meredith and Arnold Bennett, had to do his Spelling for him at 14 Bucks per.

The Cerebellum of Elam was probably about the dimensions of a Malaga Grape.

Sizing him by his Looks, one would have opined that Nature meant him for a Ticket-taker in a suburban Cinema Palace.

Elam was a mental Gnat and a spiritual Microbe, but the Geezer knew how to annex the Kale.

When Providence is directing the Handouts, she very often slips some Squarehead the canny Gift of corralling the Cush, but holds out all of the desirable Attributes supposed to distinguish Man from what you see in the Cages at the Zoo.

After the Pater had earned his Shaft in the Cemetery, Elam became the Loud Noise around a dinky Manufacturing Plant down by the Yards. The Cracker Barrel Coterie and all the Old Ladies who had become muscle-bound from wielding the Sledge predicted that Elam would put the Organization into the Ditch, wrong side up.

The Well-wishers, the Brotherly lovers, and the total membership of the Helping Hand Society sat back waiting for Elam to be dug out of the Debris, so they could collect Witness Fees at the Autopsy.

The Junior earned their abiding Dislike by putting one across.

He made the Fossils sit up in their padded Rocking Chairs and pay some attention to the Idiot Child.

He never could hold down any Position until tried out for a Captain of Industry and then he began to Bat 450 and Field 998.

After the dusty Workmen had manufactured the Product, and the Salesmen had unloaded it, and the Collectors had brought in the Dinero, then Elam had to sit at a Mahogany Desk with a Picture of Claudine in front of him, and figure how much of the hard-earned Mazuma would be doled out to his greedy Employees.

Sometimes he would be compelled to fork over nearly half the Gross, whereupon his Heart would ache and he would become Morose.

In a few Years he had a lot of new Buildings, with Skylights and improved Machinery and all sorts of humane Appliances to enable the Working Force to increase the Output.

As the Bank Account expanded and the Happy Couple found themselves going up, Claudine began to scan the Horizon and act restless-like. She said the Home Town was Impossible. It certainly did seem Contrary to Reason.

Any Woman with a salaried Husband could bust into Society if she sang in a Choir or owned an Ice-cream Freezer.

Claudine was for migrating to some high-toned Community beyond the Rising Sun, where she could sit in Marble Halls and compare Jewelry with proud Duennas of her own Station.

Seeing Claudine at the corner of 8th and Central, waiting for the Open Car, one would not have suspected that she harbored Intentions on the Court Circles of Europe.

One would merely have guessed that she was on her way to the Drug Store to purchase much Camphor.

But she had taken a peek at the Palm Rooms and the powdered Lackeys and the Tea Riot at the Plaza, and she was panting inwardly.

She wanted to hang a silver Bell around her neck and go galloping with the white-faced Thoroughbreds.

It was no good trying to work up Speed on a half-mile track in the Prairie Loam.

Once in a while Claudine made a bold Sashay to start something devilish, but the Fillies trained on the Farm did not seem gaited for the Grand Circuit.

As for the Servant Problem, it was something ferocious. City Help could not be lured to the Tall Grass, and all the Locals had been schooled at the Railway Eating-House.

Elam and Claudine had a Cook named Gusta, born somewhere near the Arctic Circle in Europe.

Her fried Chicken drowned in thick Gravy came under the head of Regular Food.

She could turn out Waffles as long as there was a Customer in sight. The Biscuits on which she specialized were light as Down.

The Things she fixed to Eat were Fine and Dandy but she never had heard of a Cuisine.

When you took her away from regular Chow and made her tackle something Casserole or En Tasse, she blew.

Also there was a Maid who should have belonged to the Stevedore's Union. She could pack Victuals in from the Buttery and slam them down on the Table, a la Commercial Hotel, but when it came to building up an intricate Design with an ingrowing Napkin, three spoons, four Knives, five forks, and all the long-stemmed Glasses, to say nothing of an artful pyramiding of Cut Flowers around the Candelabra, then she was simply a female Blacksmith.

Claudine would throw a Dinner once in a while, just to subdue the Wife and Daughter of the National Bank, but the Crew would nearly always crab the Entertainment.

With the Support accorded by the solid ivory Staff, she had a fat Chance to give a correct imitation of Mrs. Stuyvesant Fish.

All during the nine Courses she had to yelp more Orders than the Foreman of a Street Gang. A Megaphone would have helped some. The Hostess who wishes to look and carry on like a Duchess, certainly finds it vexing when pop-eyed Lizzie leans against all of the principal Guests in turn and then endeavors to shoot the Episcopalian Rector in the Neck with a gush of real Champagne.

After one of these sad Affairs, at which the Rummies had balled up the whole Menu, Claudine came to the front with an Ultimatum. She said she was going to can the awful Birthplace and spend the remainder of her Natural among the real Rowdy-Dows.

"Right-o, Babe!" spoke up Elam. "To-day I have put the Works into a new Combine which makes me a Janitor so far as the Plant is concerned, but boosts me into the Charley Schwab division when it comes to Collateral. I have three million Iron Boys and most of it is Turkey. I am foot-loose and free as a Robin. Let us beat it to the Big Show. It is about time that the vast Territory lying toward the East should be aroused from its Lethargy. Go as far as you like."

The two were foxy. For monetary and real-estate Reasons they did not give it out cold that they were making a final Getaway. They planned to have Gusta remain at the dear old Dump as a Caretaker, but it was merely a Bluff.

When the Town Hack followed a Wagon-Load of Trunks to the Depot, Claudine leaned out and said: "Fare thee well, O you Indian Village! This is the Parting of the Ways for little Sunshine."

Next we see them in the gaudy Diner, eating Sweetbreads.

Next day thousands of warm-hearted New Yorkers were packed along the Water front all the Way from the Battery to Grant's Tomb, giving royal Welcome to the Corn-fed Pilgrims. At any rate, they were Packed.

When Elam and Claudine entered the Hotel, the discerning Bell-hops had them stand back until the others had registered.

They were Important but they did not carry any Signs.

Elam should have worn the Letter of Credit on the outside.

After they had taken the Imperial Suite and invited all the Servants on the Twelfth Floor to a Silver Shower, they found that the Call-Bells worked fine. If Elam moved in the general direction of a Button, a handsome West Pointer would flit in with a pitcher of Iced Water and then hover around for his Bit.

Both realized that the first requisite was a lot of new Scenery. Even when they rapped sharply with a Spoon and ordered Garcon to hurry up the Little Birds with a Flagon of St. Regis Bubbles to come along as a drench, they realized that they did not look the Parts.

Elam still combed his Hair in the style approved by the "Barbers' Guide and Manual" for 1887.

Claudine was fully clothed as far up as her Neck and didn't have the Nerve to hoist the Lorgnette.

Elam went out and had himself draped by a swagger Tailor who was said to do a lot of Work for the Vanderbilt Boys.

In his Afternoon Wear he resembled the Manager of a Black-Goods Department.

After donning the complete Soup and Fish, known in swozzey circles as Thirteen and the Odd, he didn't look as much like a Waiter as one might have supposed. He looked more like the 'Bus who takes away the Dishes.

Claudine yielded herself up to a Modiste. The Good Woman from out of Town was a trifle Long in the Tooth at this stage of our Narrative, but Mme. Bunk convinced her that she was about half way between the Trundle Bed and her First Party.

She ordered all the Chic Novelties recommended for Flappers, so that Elam began to walk about ten feet behind her, wondering vaguely if his family was still respectable.

The new Harness and a careless habit of counting Money in Public soon gave them an enviable Reputation in the principal Cafes, although they could not observe that they were moving any nearer to the Newport Colony.

The shift from Pig's Knuckles to Ambrosia and Nectar had been a little sudden for Elam, and sometimes, when they were darting hither and thither, from Road-House to Play-House and thence to the Louis XIV Sitting-Room by way of the Tango-Joint, he would moan a little and act like a Quitter.

Whereupon Claudine would jack him up and tell him to pull out his Cuffs and push back the Forelock and try to be Human.

No use. He was strictly Ritz-Carlton from the Pumps to the Topper, but the word "Boob" was plainly stenciled on the glossy Front.

When they had conquered all the Eating-Places in the Tenderloin they moved on to Europe, where they were just as welcome as Influenza.

It was great to sit in the Savoy at the Supper Hour, surrounded by the best known people mentioned in the Court Circulars.

It was indeed a privilege for Elam and Claudine to be among the British Cousins, even if the British Cousins did not seem to place Elam and Claudine.

Looking in any direction they could see naught but frosty and forbidding Shoulder Blades.

After partaking of their Sole and Grouse and winning a pleasant "Good-Night" from the Chevalier in the Check-Room, they would escape to their Apartments and talk to the Dog.

In Paris they did better.

They learned that by going out on the Boulevard and whistling, they could summon a whole Regiment of high-born and patrician Down-and-Outers. Most of the Titles were slightly worm-eaten and spotted with Scale, but nevertheless Genuine.

It was Nuts for Claudine to assemble all of the Noblemen to be picked up around the Lobby and give them a free run and jump at the Carte du Jour.

Her Dinners soon became the talk of the Chambermaids employed at the Hotel.

Any one willing to cut loose on Caviar and stuff raised under Glass will never have to dine alone in gay Paree.

Whenever Elam made a noise like 1000 Frogs he found a lot of well-bred Connoisseurs at his Elbow, all ready to have something unusual brought up from the Cellar.

The securing of an Invitation to one of Claudine's formal Dinners was almost as difficult as getting into Luna Park.

However, the list of guests sounded Real when sent back to America and printed for the entertainment of persons living in Boarding-Houses. Claudine became slightly puffed. When she found herself between a couple of perfumed Lads wearing Medals she would give Friend Husband the Office to move to one side and curl up in the Grass and not ruin the Ensemble by butting in.

Elam was usually at the foot of the Table behind a mass of Orchids. Once in a while he would try to crowd into the Conversation just to let them know that old Ready Money was still present, but every time he came up Dearie would do her blamedest to Bean him and put him out of the Game.

Claudine could make a stab at the new Pictures in the Salon and even run nimbly around the edge of the Futurist vogue.

Elam was ready to discuss Steamship Lines or Railway Accommodations, but when he was put against the Tall Brows he began to burn low and smell of the Wick.

Often, when surfeited with Truffles, he would wonder what

had become of the Green Corn, the K. and K., the regular Chicken with Giblets, the Hot Cherry Pie, the smoking Oyster Stew, and the Smearcase with Chives, such as Gusta used to send in.

These reminders of a lowly Past were very distasteful to Claudine. Once he talked in his Sleep about Cod-fish Balls, and next morning she lit on him something ramfugious.

After the Parisian triumphs it seemed a safe bet to return home and make a new effort to mingle with the Face-Cards.

This time they took a House in New York and went after Grand Opera as if they knew what it was about.

The Son of an earl consented to Buttle for them. He refused them Butter with their Meals and kept them trembling most of the time, but they determined to do things Right, even if both died of Nervous Prostration.

When they began making real Headway and were recognized in the Park by some of the Headliners, Claudine would chide Elam for his early Doubts and Fears.

"This has got the Middle West skinned forty ways from the Jack," she would exclaim, gayly, as they motored up the Avenue. "Me for the White Lights! It's a good thing you had a Pacemaker or you would now be wearing detachable Cuffs and putting Sugar on your Lettuce."

Two years had elapsed since the escape from being Buried Alive. They were, to all outward appearances, City-broke.

One day Claudine allowed that she was tired of Bridge and the gay Routine. She announced that she was slipping away to Virginia Hot Springs to cool off and rest.

Elam said that while she was lying up, he would inspect certain Mining Properties in Canada.

He drove Honey to the train, then he tore back to the palatial Home, chucked a few Props into a Suit Case and headed for the Grand Central. He never stopped going until he ducked in the Back Way, through the Grape Arbor, past the Woodshed, into the Kitchen of the old Homestead in which he first saw the Light of Day.

Gusta nearly keeled when she lamped the long-lost Boss.

"Get busy," he said. "One fried Steak, the size of a Lap-Robe, smothered with Onions, two dozen Biscuits without any Armor Plate, one bushel of home-made Pork and Beans, much Butter, and a Gallon of Coffee in a Tureen."

"You will have to wait a while," said the faithful Gusta. "There is a double order of Ham and Turnips ahead of you. While you are waiting you might go up and call on the Missus. She has put on her old Blue Wrapper and the Yarn Slippers and is now lying on a Feather Tick in the Spare Room."

MORAL: The only City People are those born so.

THE NEW FABLE OF THE MARATHON IN THE MUD
AND THE LAUREL WREATH

A Stub-Nosed Primary Pupil, richly endowed with old-gold Freckles, lived in a one-cylinder Town, far from the corroding influences of the Stock Exchange.

He arrived during the age of Board Sidewalks, Congress Gaiters, and Pie for Breakfast.

The Paper Collar, unmindful of the approaching Celluloid, was still affected by the more tony Dressers. Prison-made Bow Ties, with the handy elastic Fastener, were then considered right Natty.

Limousines, Eugenics, Appendicitis, and the regulation of Combines were beyond the rise of the Hill, so the talk was mostly about the Weather and Married Women.

The baptismal Cognomen of the mottled Offspring was Alexander Campbell Purvis, but on account of his sunny Disposition he was known to the Countryside as Aleck.

One morning the Lad did his crawl from under the Quilt at an hour when our Best People of the new Century are sending away the empty Siphons. He was acting on a Hunch.

The far-famed Yankee Robinson show, with the Trick Mule and the smiling Tumblers, had exhibited the day before on the vacant Lot between the Grist-Mill and the Parsonage.

Aleck was familiar with the juvenile Tradition that Treasure could be discovered at or near the trampled Spot on which the Ticket-Wagon had been anchored.

It was known that the agitated Yahoos from up in Catfish Country were likely to fumble and spill their saved-up Currency, thereby avoiding the trouble of handing it over to the Grafters later on.

Aleck was the first Prospector to show. He got busy and uncovered a Silver Buck.

It looked about the size of a Ferris Wheel.

While beating it for the parental Roof he began laying out in his Mind all the Pleasures of the Flesh that he could command with the Mass of Lucre.

The miscue he made was to flash his Fortune in the Family Circle. After breakfast he found himself being steered to the Farmers & Merchants' Bank.

He was pried away from the Cart-Wheel and given a teeny little Book which showed that he was a Depositor.

"Now, Alexander C.," said his Ma, "if you will shin up the ladder and pick Cherries every day this week at two cents per Quart, by nightfall of Saturday you will have another Case-Note to put into Cold Storage."

"But, if I continue dropping the proceeds of my Labor into the Reservoir, what is there in it for me?" asked the inquisitive Chick.

His mother replied, "Why, you will have the Gratification of moving up to the Window at the Bank and earning a Smile of Approbation from old Mr. Fishberry with the Throat Whiskers."

So the aspiring Manikin clung to the perilous Tree-Tops day after day, dropping the ruby Cherries into the suspended Bucket, while all of the Relatives stood on the ground and applauded.

One day there was a Conference and it was discovered that little Aleck was solvent to the extent of $2.80.

"Would it not be Rayzorius?" queried the Sire of Alexander; "would it not be Ipskalene if Aleck kept on and on until he had assembled five whole Dollars?"

Thus spurred to Endeavor by a large and rooting Gallery, the Urchin went prowling for Old Iron, which he trundled off to the Junkman.

Also for empty Bottles, which he laboriously scoured and delivered at the Drug Store for a mere dribble of Chicken Feed.

The sheet of Copper brought a tidy Sum, while old Mrs. Arbuckle wondered what had become of her Wash-Boiler.

With a V to his Credit, Aleck put a Padlock on every Pocket in his Store Suit and went Money-Mad.

He acquired a Runt and swilled it with solicitude until the Butcher made him an offer.

It was a proud Moment when he eased in the $7.60 to T. W. Fishberry, who told him to keep on scrounging and some day he would own a share in the Building & Loan.

Our Hero fooled away his time in School until he was all of eleven years old, when he became associated with one Blodgett in the Grocery Business, at a weekly Insult of Two Bones.

All the time Aleck was cleaning the Coal-Oil Lamps or watching the New Orleans Syrup trickle into the Jug, he was figuring how much of the Stipend he could segregate and isolate and set aside for the venerable Mr. Fishberry, the Taker-In up at the Bank with the Chinchilla on the Larynx.

For ten long years the White Slave tested Eggs and scooped the C Sugar. When Aleck became of Age, Mr. Blodgett was compelling him to take $30 the first of every month.

He lived on Snowballs in the Winter and Dandelions in the Summer, but he had paid $800 on a two-story Brick facing Railroad Street.

His name was a Byword and Hissing among the Pool-Players.

Nevertheless, he stood Ace High with the old Two-per-cent-a-Month up at the Abattoir known as the Farmers & Merchants' Bank.

The Boys who dropped in every thirty Days came to know him as a Wise Fish and a Close Buyer. They boosted at Headquarters, so the first thing you know Aleck was a Drummer, with two Grips bigger than Dog-Houses and a chance to swing on the Expense Account.

A lowly and unsung Wanamaker would be sitting in his Prunery, wearing Yarn Wristlets to keep warm and meditating another Attack on the Bottle of Stomach Bitters in the Safe, when Aleck would breeze in and light on him and sell him several Gross of something he didn't need.

The Traveling Salesman dug up many a Cross-Roads overlooked by the Map-Makers.

He knew how to pin a Rube against the Wall and make him say "Yes."

He rode in Cabooses, fought the Roller-Towels, endured the Taunts of Ess, Bess, and Tess who shot the Sody Biscuit, and reclined in the Chamber of Horrors, entirely surrounded by

Wall-Paper, but what cared he?

He was salting the Spon.

He was closing in on the Needful.

For a term of years he lived on Time-Tables and slept sitting up.

Day after day he dog-trotted through a feverish Routine of unpacking and packing, and then climbing back to the superheated Day Coach among the curdled Smells.

Every January 1st he did a Gaspard Chuckle when he checked up the total Get, for now he owned two Brick Buildings and had tasted a little Blood in the way of Chattel Mortgages.

One of the partners in the Jobbing Concern happened to die. Before Rigor Mortis could set in or the Undertaker had time to flash a Tape Measure, Aleck was up at the grief-stricken Home to cop out an Option on the Interest.

Now he could give the Cackle to all the Knights of the Road who had blown their Substance along the gay White Ways of Crawfordsville, Bucyrus, and Sedalia.

He was the real Gazook with a Glass Cage, a sliding Desk and a whole Battery of Rubber Stamps.

In order to learn every Kink of the Game, freeze out the other Holders of Stock and gradually possess himself of all the Money in the World, Aleck now found it necessary to organize himself into both a Day and a Night Shift and have his Lunches brought in.

The various Smoothenheimers who were out on the Road had a proud chance to get by with the padded Expense Account. Aleck could smell a Phoney before he opened the Envelope, because that is how he got His.

With a three-ton Burden on his aching Shoulders, he staggered up the flinty Incline.

Away back yonder, while sleeping above the Store, a vision had come to him. He saw himself sitting as a Director at a Bank Meeting—an enlarged and glorified Fishberry.

Now he was playing Fox and pulling for the Dream to work out.

The cold-eyed Custodians up at the main Fortress of Credit began to take notice of the Rustler.

He was a Glutton for Punishment, a Discounter from away back, and a Demon for applying the Acid Test to every Account.

He was a Sure-Thinger, air-tight and playing naught but Cinches. No wonder they all took a slant at him and spotted him as a Comer.

The Business Associates of Alexander liked to see Europe from the inside every summer and investigate the Cocktail Crop of Florida every winter, so they allowed him to be the Works.

He began building the Skids which finally carried them to the Fresh Air and left only one name on the Gold Sign.

Up to his Chin in Debt and with a Panic looming on the Horizon, it behooved Alexander to be on the job at 7:30 A. M. and hang around to scan the Pay-Roll until 9:30 P. M.

Ofttimes while galloping from his Apartment to the Galleys or chasing homeward to grab off a few wasteful hours of Slumber, he would see People of the Lower Classes going out to the Parks with Picnic Baskets, or lined up at the Vaudeville Palaces, or watching a hard-faced Soubrette demonstrate something in a Show Window.

It got him to think Dubs could frivol around and waste the golden Moments when they might be hopping on to a Ten-Cent Piece.

His usual Gait was that of a man going for the Doctor, and he talked Numbers to himself as he sped along and mumbled over the im portantLetters he was about to dictate.

Those who were pushed out of his way would overhear a scrap or two of the Raving and think he was Balmy.

The answer is that every hard-working Business Guy acts as if he had Screech-Owls in the Tower.

Aleck had his whole Staff so buffaloed that the Hirelings tried to keep up with him, so that Life in the Beehive was just one thing after another, with no Intermission.

The Whip cracked every five minutes, and the Help would dig in their toes and take a fresh lean-up against the Collars, for the Main Squeeze was trying to be a Bank Director, and Rockefeller had stolen a long start on him.

With a thousand important Details claiming his attention, Aleck had no time to monkey with side issues such as the general State of his Health or the multifarious plans for uplifting the Flat-Heads that he could see from his Window.

Those who recommended Golf to him seemed to forget that no one ever laid by anything while on the Links.

As for the Plain People, his only Conviction when he surveyed them in the Mass was that every Man-Jack was holding back Money that rightfully belonged to him (Alexander).

Needless to say, the battling Financier was made welcome at the Director's Table and handed a piece of a Trust Company and became an honored Guest when any Melon was to be sliced.

All that he dreamt while sleeping in the cold room over the Store had eventuated for fair.

The more Irons in the Fire, the more flip-flops he turned.

He never paused, except to weep over the fact that some of the rival Procurers were getting more than he could show. It was an unjust World. Brushing away the salty Tears, he would leap seven feet into the Air and spear a passing Dollar.

By the time he had the Million necessary for the support of a suitable and well-recommended Lady, he was too busy to go chasing and too foxy to split his Pile with a rank Outsider.

His Motor-Car squawked at the Sparrow Cops when they waved their Arms.

The engineer who pulled the Private Car always had his Orders to hit it up.

Sometimes the Private Secretary would drop out from Exhaustion, but the Human Dynamo never slowed up. He would shout his General Orders into the Cylinder of a Talking Machine.

He reposed at Night with a Ticker on his Bosom and a Receiver at his Ear.

When he finally flew the Track and blew out the Carburetor, they had to use a Net to get him under Control so that he could be carted away to the Hospital.

Then the Trained Nurse had to practice all the Trick Holds known to Frank Gotch to keep him from arising to resume the grim Battle against his Enemies on the Board.

He fluttered long before calming down, but finally they got him all spread out and as nice a Patient as one could wish to see.

When he was too weak to start anything, Doc sat down and cheered him along by telling what Precautions should have been taken, along about 1880.

"And now, I have some News for you," said the Practitioner, holding in his Grief so well that no one could notice it. "You are going away from here. Owing to the total absence of many Organs commonly regarded as essential, it will be impossible for you to go back to the Desk and duplicate any of your notable Stunts. No doubt we shall be able to engage Six Men of Presentable Appearance to act as Pall-Bearers. It is our purpose to proceed to the Cemetery by Automobile so as not to impede Traffic on any of the Surface Lines in which you are so heavily interested. I congratulate you on getting so far along before being tripped up, and I am wondering if you have a Final Request to make."

"Just one," replied the Great Man, "I'd like to have you or somebody else tell me what it's all been about."

The only remaining Fact to be chronicled is that the original Dollar, picked up on the Circus Lot, was found among the Effects.

A Nephew, whom Alexander Campbell Purvis never had seen, took the Dollar and with it purchased two Packs of Egyptian Cigaroots, Regal size, with Gold Tips.

MORAL: A pinch of Change, carefully put by, always comes in handy.

THE END

ABOUT THE AUTHOR

 George Ade (February 9, 1866 - May 16, 1944) was an American writer, newspaper columnist, and playwright.

Ade was born in Kentland, Indiana, one of seven children raised by John and Adaline (Bush) Ade. He graduated from Purdue University in 1887. Lafayette, Indiana is where he met and started a lifelong friendship with cartoonist and Sigma Chi brother John T. McCutcheon. Ade worked as a reporter for the Lafayette Call.

In 1890 Ade joined the Chicago Morning News, which later became the Chicago Record, where McCutcheon was working. He wrote the column, Stories of the Streets and of the Town. In the column, which McCutcheon illustrated, George Ade illustrated Chicago-life. It featured characters like Artie, an office boy; Doc Horne, a gentlemanly liar; and Pink Marsh, a black shoeshine boy. Ade's well-known "fables in slang" also made their first appearance in this popular column.

Ade's literary reputation rests upon his achievements as a great humorist of American character during an important era in American history: the first large wave of migration from the countryside to burgeoning cities like Chicago, where, in fact, Ade produced his best fiction.

Choose from Thousands of 1stWorldLibrary Classics By

A. M. Barnard	Booth Tarkington	Edward Everett Hale
Ada Leverson	Boyd Cable	Edward J. O'Biren
Adolphus William Ward	Bram Stoker	Edward S. Ellis
Aesop	C. Collodi	Edwin L. Arnold
Agatha Christie	C. E. Orr	Eleanor Atkins
Alexander Aaronsohn	C. M. Ingleby	Eleanor Hallowell Abbott
Alexander Kielland	Carolyn Wells	Eliot Gregory
Alexandre Dumas	Catherine Parr Traill	Elizabeth Gaskell
Alfred Gatty	Charles A. Eastman	Elizabeth McCracken
Alfred Ollivant	Charles Amory Beach	Elizabeth Von Arnim
Alice Duer Miller	Charles Dickens	Ellem Key
Alice Turner Curtis	Charles Dudley Warner	Emerson Hough
Alice Dunbar	Charles Farrar Browne	Emilie F. Carlen
Allen Chapman	Charles Ives	Emily Bronte
Alleyne Ireland	Charles Kingsley	Emily Dickinson
Ambrose Bierce	Charles Klein	Enid Bagnold
Amelia E. Barr	Charles Hanson Towne	Enilor Macartney Lane
Amory H. Bradford	Charles Lathrop Pack	Erasmus W. Jones
Andrew Lang	Charles Romyn Dake	Ernie Howard Pie
Andrew McFarland Davis	Charles Whibley	Ethel May Dell
Andy Adams	Charles Willing Beale	Ethel Turner
Angela Brazil	Charlotte M. Braeme	Ethel Watts Mumford
Anna Alice Chapin	Charlotte M. Yonge	Eugene Sue
Anna Sewell	Charlotte Perkins Stetson	Eugenie Foa
Annie Besant	Clair W. Hayes	Eugene Wood
Annie Hamilton Donnell	Clarence Day Jr.	Eustace Hale Ball
Annie Payson Call	Clarence E. Mulford	Evelyn Everett-green
Annie Roe Carr	Clemence Housman	Everard Cotes
Annonaymous	Confucius	F. H. Cheley
Anton Chekhov	Coningsby Dawson	F. J. Cross
Archibald Lee Fletcher	Cornelis DeWitt Wilcox	F. Marion Crawford
Arnold Bennett	Cyril Burleigh	Fannie E. Newberry
Arthur C. Benson	D. H. Lawrence	Federick Austin Ogg
Arthur Conan Doyle	Daniel Defoe	Ferdinand Ossendowski
Arthur M. Winfield	David Garnett	Fergus Hume
Arthur Ransome	Dinah Craik	Florence A. Kilpatrick
Arthur Schnitzler	Don Carlos Janes	Fremont B. Deering
Arthur Train	Donald Keyhoe	Francis Bacon
Atticus	Dorothy Kilner	Francis Darwin
B.H. Baden-Powell	Dougan Clark	Frances Hodgson Burnett
B. M. Bower	Douglas Fairbanks	Frances Parkinson Keyes
B. C. Chatterjee	E. Nesbit	Frank Gee Patchin
Baroness Emmuska Orczy	E. P. Roe	Frank Harris
Baroness Orczy	E. Phillips Oppenheim	Frank Jewett Mather
Basil King	E. S. Brooks	Frank L. Packard
Bayard Taylor	Earl Barnes	Frank V. Webster
Ben Macomber	Edgar Rice Burroughs	Frederic Stewart Isham
Bertha Muzzy Bower	Edith Van Dyne	Frederick Trevor Hill
Bjornstjerne Bjornson	Edith Wharton	Frederick Winslow Taylor

Friedrich Kerst
Friedrich Nietzsche
Fyodor Dostoyevsky
G.A. Henty
G.K. Chesterton
Gabrielle E. Jackson
Garrett P. Serviss
Gaston Leroux
George A. Warren
George Ade
Geroge Bernard Shaw
George Cary Eggleston
George Durston
George Ebers
George Eliot
George Gissing
George MacDonald
George Meredith
George Orwell
George Sylvester Viereck
George Tucker
George W. Cable
George Wharton James
Gertrude Atherton
Gordon Casserly
Grace E. King
Grace Gallatin
Grace Greenwood
Grant Allen
Guillermo A. Sherwell
Gulielma Zollinger
Gustav Flaubert
H. A. Cody
H. B. Irving
H.C. Bailey
H. G. Wells
H. H. Munro
H. Irving Hancock
H. R. Naylor
H. Rider Haggard
H. W. C. Davis
Haldeman Julius
Hall Caine
Hamilton Wright Mabie
Hans Christian Andersen
Harold Avery
Harold McGrath
Harriet Beecher Stowe
Harry Castlemon
Harry Coghill
Harry Houidini

Hayden Carruth
Helent Hunt Jackson
Helen Nicolay
Hendrik Conscience
Hendy David Thoreau
Henri Barbusse
Henrik Ibsen
Henry Adams
Henry Ford
Henry Frost
Henry James
Henry Jones Ford
Henry Seton Merriman
Henry W Longfellow
Herbert A. Giles
Herbert Carter
Herbert N. Casson
Herman Hesse
Hildegard G. Frey
Homer
Honore De Balzac
Horace B. Day
Horace Walpole
Horatio Alger Jr.
Howard Pyle
Howard R. Garis
Hugh Lofting
Hugh Walpole
Humphry Ward
Ian Maclaren
Inez Haynes Gillmore
Irving Bacheller
Isabel Cecilia Williams
Isabel Hornibrook
Israel Abrahams
Ivan Turgenev
J.G.Austin
J. Henri Fabre
J. M. Barrie
J. M. Walsh
J. Macdonald Oxley
J. R. Miller
J. S. Fletcher
J. S. Knowles
J. Storer Clouston
J. W. Duffield
Jack London
Jacob Abbott
James Allen
James Andrews
James Baldwin

James Branch Cabell
James DeMille
James Joyce
James Lane Allen
James Lane Allen
James Oliver Curwood
James Oppenheim
James Otis
James R. Driscoll
Jane Abbott
Jane Austen
Jane L. Stewart
Janet Aldridge
Jens Peter Jacobsen
Jerome K. Jerome
Jessie Graham Flower
John Buchan
John Burroughs
John Cournos
John F. Kennedy
John Gay
John Glasworthy
John Habberton
John Joy Bell
John Kendrick Bangs
John Milton
John Philip Sousa
John Taintor Foote
Jonas Lauritz Idemil Lie
Jonathan Swift
Joseph A. Altsheler
Joseph Carey
Joseph Conrad
Joseph E. Badger Jr
Joseph Hergesheimer
Joseph Jacobs
Jules Vernes
Julian Hawthrone
Julie A Lippmann
Justin Huntly McCarthy
Kakuzo Okakura
Karle Wilson Baker
Kate Chopin
Kenneth Grahame
Kenneth McGaffey
Kate Langley Bosher
Kate Langley Bosher
Katherine Cecil Thurston
Katherine Stokes
L. A. Abbot
L. T. Meade

L. Frank Baum
Latta Griswold
Laura Dent Crane
Laura Lee Hope
Laurence Housman
Lawrence Beasley
Leo Tolstoy
Leonid Andreyev
Lewis Carroll
Lewis Sperry Chafer
Lilian Bell
Lloyd Osbourne
Louis Hughes
Louis Joseph Vance
Louis Tracy
Louisa May Alcott
Lucy Fitch Perkins
Lucy Maud Montgomery
Luther Benson
Lydia Miller Middleton
Lyndon Orr
M. Corvus
M. H. Adams
Margaret E. Sangster
Margret Howth
Margaret Vandercook
Margaret W. Hungerford
Margret Penrose
Maria Edgeworth
Maria Thompson Daviess
Mariano Azuela
Marion Polk Angellotti
Mark Overton
Mark Twain
Mary Austin
Mary Catherine Crowley
Mary Cole
Mary Hastings Bradley
Mary Roberts Rinehart
Mary Rowlandson
M. Wollstonecraft Shelley
Maud Lindsay
Max Beerbohm
Myra Kelly
Nathaniel Hawthrone
Nicolo Machiavelli
O. F. Walton
Oscar Wilde

Owen Johnson
P.G. Wodehouse
Paul and Mabel Thorne
Paul G. Tomlinson
Paul Severing
Percy Brebner
Percy Keese Fitzhugh
Peter B. Kyne
Plato
Quincy Allen
R. Derby Holmes
R. L. Stevenson
R. S. Ball
Rabindranath Tagore
Rahul Alvares
Ralph Bonehill
Ralph Henry Barbour
Ralph Victor
Ralph Waldo Emmerson
Rene Descartes
Ray Cummings
Rex Beach
Rex E. Beach
Richard Harding Davis
Richard Jefferies
Richard Le Gallienne
Robert Barr
Robert Frost
Robert Gordon Anderson
Robert L. Drake
Robert Lansing
Robert Lynd
Robert Michael Ballantyne
Robert W. Chambers
Rosa Nouchette Carey
Rudyard Kipling
Saint Augustine
Samuel B. Allison
Samuel Hopkins Adams
Sarah Bernhardt
Sarah C. Hallowell
Selma Lagerlof
Sherwood Anderson
Sigmund Freud
Standish O'Grady
Stanley Weyman
Stella Benson
Stella M. Francis

Stephen Crane
Stewart Edward White
Stijn Streuvels
Swami Abhedananda
Swami Parmananda
T. S. Ackland
T. S. Arthur
The Princess Der Ling
Thomas A. Janvier
Thomas A Kempis
Thomas Anderton
Thomas Bailey Aldrich
Thomas Bulfinch
Thomas De Quincey
Thomas Dixon
Thomas H. Huxley
Thomas Hardy
Thomas More
Thornton W. Burgess
U. S. Grant
Upton Sinclair
Valentine Williams
Various Authors
Vaughan Kester
Victor Appleton
Victor G. Durham
Victoria Cross
Virginia Woolf
Wadsworth Camp
Walter Camp
Walter Scott
Washington Irving
Wilbur Lawton
Wilkie Collins
Willa Cather
Willard F. Baker
William Dean Howells
William le Queux
W. Makepeace Thackeray
William W. Walter
William Shakespeare
Winston Churchill
Yei Theodora Ozaki
Yogi Ramacharaka
Young E. Allison
Zane Grey

www.ingramcontent.com/pod-product-compliance
Lightning Source LLC
Chambersburg PA
CBHW051834170626
46807CB00003B/1177